ways to go

KATRINA MARIE

Editor: Small Edits

Cover Design: KP Design

This book is for those wanting a second chance, you are worthy of it.

THE STREETS of Asheville are bustling. People are walking down the street staring into shop windows as if they don't have a care in the world. I wish I could say the same. I wish guilt didn't eat away at me, especially now, as I watch Tonya and Reaf walking down the sidewalk holding hands.

That should be me. I should be the one with my arms wrapped around Tonya and focusing on our baby girl. But...she chose him. I can understand why, but it doesn't stop the jealousy from bubbling up in my gut. It doesn't keep the anger from rising to the surface. I knew what I would see if I came home from school, but I still decided to come back and torture myself by watching them together. Asheville is a small town, and there's no way I would be able to avoid them completely.

Tonya and Reaf stroll down Main Street, glancing through shop windows, pushing a stroller in front of them. A stroller that holds my child. My beautiful baby girl, Layla. I really don't have any right to call her mine. I mean, she is biologically, but I haven't been here for her or Tonya. At least, not in any way that put me in a good light. I gave up that right when I asked Tonya to give me time to adjust to the knowledge that I have a child.

They stop in front of a baby boutique, hands pressed to their foreheads, trying to see through the glare in the window. Reaf bends down, and when he stands up again, he has Layla cuddled up against his chest. I don't know what they are shopping for, but I'm not a fan of how cozy they look together.

I clench my hands together until they are curled into fists. I can feel my face heating, and my breathing is becoming labored. I'm struggling to get my anger under control, but it's hard. I shouldn't be this enraged, but that's my kid he's holding. My kid he's playing father to.

I quickly turn the corner putting them out of my line of sight. I need to calm down, but I know seeing them together, as a *family*, isn't going to accomplish anything. I shouldn't have come back. I could be in my dorm right now playing Madden with the guys. But, no...I'm storming off like a fucking child because I can't handle the repercussions of my decision to not be in Layla's life yet.

I wasn't ready for that responsibility. Hell, I'm still not ready but I want to be. Not only for Layla but for myself. I want to have the strength to do this whole co-parenting thing that Tonya kept on about.

I shove my way through people milling about enjoying their Spring day, while I'm in turmoil. I'm pretty sure I hear someone holler my name, but I don't turn around. If Tonya is chasing after me, I won't be able to handle it.

Finally seeing the outline of my car, I pick up the pace. Hitting the key fob at the same time as I grab the handle, I yank the door open and slide into the car. I check both ways before pulling out of the parking spot and into traffic.

In my rearview mirror I see Tonya standing at the edge of the sidewalk disbelief written all over her face. I feel a stab of guilt that I've hurt her once again, but there's nothing I can do about it. I'm going to run home, grab my stuff and head back to the dorms. I'm not ready to face this.

jake

TOSSING my bag onto the bed, I examine my room. I'm not sure what I'm expecting, it all looks exactly the same as it did when I hauled ass out of Asheville in the middle of Spring Break. My bed is neatly made, corners tucked in, with the afghan my grandmother knitted folded at the bottom. My football trophies line the shelves on the light brown wall adjacent to my bed, and my desk sits empty except for a few pieces of paper stacked neatly in the corner.

I grimace when I take it all in. I assumed my parents would have repurposed, or at least repainted, this room. It's not like I'm here all that much. I'd be perfectly fine sleeping in the guest room, but it appears they want to keep my childhood room exactly like it is, stuck in a weird sort of time capsule.

Luckily, neither of them are home right now, and I couldn't be more grateful. The in-person lecture about taking off when I was last home can be put off for just a bit longer. To say they weren't amused with my sudden need to leave is an understatement. They don't under-stand why I allowed Tonya to affect me.

But, they don't understand. They were married for a few years before they had me. As soon as they found out Tonya was pregnant they wrote her off as a troubled girl that should have known better. Apparently in the eyes of Mom and Dad, it only takes one to get pregnant. I can't help rolling my eyes at the thought. The real reason they are pissed is because we aren't together anymore, and I asked for time. They are more worried about how that makes them look than they are about the well-being of their grandchild.

I'm not sure how they even sleep at night without a care in the world about how Layla is doing. People may think I'm living the dream at school, but they would be wrong. I spend most nights regretting my choices. Wondering if things would be different had I not been such an asshole to Tonya for so long, even when I was trying to get her to take me back.

Pulling my phone out of my pocket, I sit on the edge of my bed, the mattress dipping under my weight. There's nothing to do here. This town is too damn small. I'm pulling up my contacts when I get a notification that Tonya has shared something on her Facebook profile. Call me a stalker, I don't really care.

I pull up the app to see what Tonya has posted today. The first image is Layla sitting in a baby swing with the biggest, toothless, smile I've ever seen. I feel a stab of pain in my gut, wishing I was there to see it in person. I scroll further down and want to throw my phone across the room. It's a picture of Layla, Tonya and

Reaf cuddled together on the hammock her parents have in their backyard. The caption says *"ready for summer fun."*

It's almost like she is trying to shove her happiness in my face. I know that's ridiculous. She doesn't do it on purpose, but it's a sucker punch just the same. I don't have anywhere to run away to this summer. I'm going to have to deal with this eventually. But not right now. I'm going to take a nap and see what the guys are up to tonight. There's no use sitting in my room moping over something I can't control.

"This town sucks," I groan into my beer. There's absolutely nothing to do here. We could go to Dallas, but it's not like we could drink anywhere there. I just want to forget. I don't want to feel anything right now. We end up in one of the fields we used to throw our high school parties in. The same spot where I screwed up and Tonya walked out of my life.

My mood didn't improve after the nap. I'm still groggy and frustrated over the whole situation. Maybe frustration isn't the right word, it's more fear than anything else. How am I supposed to face Tonya and her new little family unit? I'm going to have to figure something out or this summer is going to be a game of evasion.

"Dude, what the hell is wrong with you?" Dylan yells from the fire pit. "You're being all dramatic staring off into space."

"Nothing, man," I reply. "Just thinking about some stuff."

Randall jumps in. "Please don't tell me you're thinking about *her*."

I jump off the truck's tailgate, beer sloshing out of the can and over my hand. Damn, that's all I need is to smell like booze when I finally make it home.

"Lay off him, Randall," Marshall calls out. "He has a lot of shit he's gotta deal with."

"I don't think anyone asked for your input, Marsh," Randall shoots back.

I'm not exactly sure how my group of friends actually functions. We're all so different from each other. Well, Marshall is definitely the most mature. I think the rest of us have some growing up to do. These guys have my back, even when they are giving me hell.

"Shut up, guys. I'm capable of dealing with my own problems. I don't really need your opinions." I rub my hand across my forehead, but not before seeing Marshall's shoulders sag in defeat. He's the only one who told me what an ass I was being to Tonya. It used to bug me because I thought he had a thing for her, but really, he's the only person that's brave enough to call me on my bullshit. I just don't take his advice very often.

Dylan is busy trying to get a fire started. He's hunched over, strategically placing small limbs on top of each other. "You got a lighter?" He asks.

"Um, no," I answer. I'm not sure why he thinks I would have one, I don't smoke. "Why are you building a fire anyway? It's too damn hot for that shit."

"So, we have some sort of light, dumbass," he argues.

"I'm all for being one with nature, but I'm not taking my chances on not being able to see the animals that come out at night."

"Pansy," I mutter, taking another swig of my beer. I won't admit it, but I completely agree with him. I want the light, but not the heat that comes with it. The air is already hot and heavy, a sign that we're probably about to get a summer storm.

That realization sends a pang of sadness through me. Tonya and I loved watching the storms roll in, especially at night. We would park down an abandoned gravel road and watch the lighting spark through the sky. My arms wrapped around her while she leaned against my chest, Brantley Gilbert or Dustin Lynch crooning through the speakers, admiring the storm raging around us.

I chug the rest of my beer, tossing the empty can in the bed of the truck, and grab another one. I'm halfway finished with this can before I signal Marshall to toss me another one. He raises his eyebrow, silently questioning me. I nod, reaching my hand out to accept the new can. The need to drown out the pain right now is more important than the hangover I'll have tomorrow.

A few hours have passed. The fire is slowly dying down, the crickets are chirping, and we can see glimmers of lightning in the distance. It's been great catching up with the guys. We've played football together for as long as I can remember, from peewee all the way through high school. Then we went our separate ways. The only person who checked up on me was Marshall, but only to make sure I wasn't doing anything stupid. He's the brother I never had.

We're also very drunk, except for Marshall since he's the responsible one. We start cleaning up our mess. We don't want to lose access to this field. The owner doesn't really care if we use it as long as we pick up afterward.

Just as I'm throwing the last of the cans in a bag in the bed of the truck, Dylan yells, "Let's get tattoos."

Marshall is already shaking his head. I can't tell if he's amused or frustrated. "That's probably not a good idea."

I feel bad for the guy. He usually ends up being the one that babysits our drunk asses. I need to work on being a better friend to him. Maybe that will help me figure out how to be a part of Layla's life.

I'm just drunk enough to agree with Dylan. "Hell yeah, let's do this."

"There's no point trying to talk y'all out of this, is there?" Marshall asks.

Randall pipes in, "Nope. Might as well get in the truck and start driving it toward Dallas."

We all pile into his truck. The seats are leather, and sticky from the Texas heat. Marshall turns on the radio, and Sam Hunt is singing about cruising down a dirt road. This night is about to get interesting.

It only takes us about thirty minutes to get to south-east Dallas. Music can be heard drifting out of bars, some of them from a stereo system while others are live. There are people all over the sidewalks, bar hopping, and finding restaurants that are still open to fill their late-night appetites.

We pull into a parking lot, paying the fee, and stumble out of the truck. We have no idea where we should go, so we start walking, joining the throngs of people. We pass tattoo shop after tattoo shop before coming to one called Life in Ink.

We peek inside in the windows and it doesn't look like they are too busy. Dylan opens the door while Marshall hangs back to make sure we aren't getting into any trouble. I know I shouldn't do this. I know it could get me into trouble with my coaches. Right now, all that matters is doing this with my friends. If we're going to do something stupid, we might as well do it together.

charleigh

IT'S BEEN A SLOW NIGHT, which is a rare thing. There are people walking in front of our shop. I can see them through the dingy glass lining our store front. Life in Ink isn't one of the huge tattoo shops everyone hears about, but we usually have a lot more traffic than this.

It's depressing. How am I supposed to become a full-fledged tattoo artist when I don't have a clientele to practice on? It's something I've always wanted to do, thanks to my uncle Corey. He's the one who instilled the love of art in me. He's also the one that would let me sit in his shop, the one I'm standing in now, and watch him work. I remember being in awe as he drew these permanent images on someone's skin, and how happy it made them when he was finished.

Not all of them were meaningful. Some people got tattoos on a bet or chose something that had absolutely no meaning to them whatsoever. But you could tell the ones that truly loved the art of tattoo. The ones that loved having pieces of their journey, their story, inked on them as a permanent reminder that they weren't the same person they were before. Those are the tattoos I want to do.

I'm about to call Corey to the front and ask him if I'm good to go home when three guys come stumbling through the door. Well, four, but one of them obviously isn't drunk off his ass. He has the good sense to be somewhat embarrassed by his friends' behavior.

"Corey," I yell to the back, this time for entirely different reasons. I have a feeling it's about to be a long night. He's going to have to handle these guys.

"How can I help you, gentlemen?" I ask, sugary sweet. Inside I'm rolling my eyes, hoping the sober friend talks some sense into these idiots and they leave. I'm not sure I have the patience to deal with any of them.

Sadly, luck is not on my side. They saunter up to the counter like they have all the time in the world. I tap my pencil on the notepad in front of me. I was in the middle of a drawing. One that I have no doubt my uncle is going to shoot down as crap. Nothing is good enough to him. I mean, I get it. I have to earn my place. But does he have to insist that everything I've done is no good? I've scoured my drawings for hours, and I can't find what I've done wrong.

"W-we would like to get a tattoo," one of them stutters. I hate when we get the inebriated ones. It makes everything so much harder.

"Do you know what you want?" I ask, seeing which artists are open. Adrian just finished up a sleeve, but I don't want to pawn the drunkards onto him. I glance over to Bianca's area, smirking. She's sitting in the chair she uses for her clients, filing her bright red nails. She's had it out for me since I started my apprenticeship. I don't know what I did to piss her off, but she's about to get this group for constantly giving me shit.

"Um, hello?" The guy with blond hair cuts into my thoughts. I must have been focusing on Bianca a little too hard. I didn't even hear what ridiculous tattoos they want to get. I already know whatever they're getting isn't going to be genuine.

"Sorry, I'll need your I.D., and you'll need to fill out these forms. Are you all getting tattoos?" I ask as I pull out the forms from under the counter. I place four forms on top of the surface and dig around in the basket that sits next to the tray holding the forms for a pen.

The sober one starts speaking, "I don't think-," but his friends quickly cut him off.

"Yes, we're all getting a tattoo," the surly guy with dark hair says before patting his friend on the back.

"Let me guess," I say. "You're all going to get cutesy matching tattoos like the girls that come in here do." I roll my eyes, and I know they don't miss the sarcasm because they're staring at me with wide grins.

The blond-haired guy raises his head, "Actually, no. Just because we came together doesn't mean we're getting the same thing."

I glance down at the form he's been filling out. His name is Jake, and not two minutes ago he looked and sounded like he was drunk out of his mind. Now he sounds as sober as the guy that lead them into the shop.

I'm about to make another sarcastic comment when Uncle Corey appears out of nowhere. "You called?"

I groan, "Yep. What took you so long? I know you didn't have any clients back there."

"I was finishing my dinner, not that it matters. This is my shop." I don't miss the wink he throws to Jake and his friends, like he's letting them in on a little secret.

I roll my eyes. I can't help it. It's my automatic reaction when Corey is being cheesy, or downright ridiculous.

Corey clears his throat. "What can I help you gentlemen with this evening?"

Even though I'm pretty sure Jake *is* drunk, he answers for all of them. "All of us want to get a tattoo." He nods at each of his friends. "Nothing big. A few of us have to be able to hide it during football season."

This is the perfect time for me to insert myself into the conversation. "I was just about to set them all up with Bianca."

Corey looks at me, puzzled. "Why? There's four of them, and four of us."

Now it's my turn to be confused. My eyebrows are furrowed, and my nose is scrunched up. I'm pretty sure my brows are almost touching. "Noooo," I drawl out. "There are only three of you, unless you have another artist hiding in your pocket."

My uncle glances at me, then the group of guys huddled in front of the counter, before pulling me off to the side. He lowers his voice, "There are four of us. I'm letting you tattoo tonight."

"Now," I shriek, and try my best to bring my voice

down a few decibels. "You want me to start tattooing tonight. With this bunch of drunk idiots."

"It's the perfect time for you to practice," he counters, looking at Jake and his friends once again. "I know that blond guy puts on a pretty good sober face, but I know pretty much everyone in that group has been drinking. They won't care if you happen to screw up. Just make sure you don't."

The word "duh" is on the tip of my tongue, but Corey continues. "Always take pride in your work. Even if the people getting it won't give it the appreciation it deserves."

That's as close to praise as I'm going to get from my uncle. Finally, after two years of cleaning the shop, setting up appointments, and showing them I know how to operate everything, I'm getting my chance.

It's not the way I envisioned starting my career, but I'll take it. I groan when Corey ushers Jake into the empty chair sitting in the area he has held for me these past two years.

I grab my sketch pad. "So, what kind of tattoo do you want?"

Jake shrugs his shoulders. "I don't know." Lifting a finger to tap his chin, he sits in silence drawing it out to grate on my nerves. "Surprise me." The smugness in his voice and posture make me want to slap him.

Ugh. "Okay," I reply.

I put pencil to paper and start drawing the most ridiculous tattoo a guy his age could get. I'll take pride in what I do, but this guy in particular gets under my skin. We'll see how he likes his surprise tattoo.

jake

"UGH," I groan. I roll over onto my stomach, pulling the pillow over my head. Hoping to get just a few more minutes of sleep. I feel like death. I'm pretty sure I look like it, too.

I glance at the wall trying to figure out what time it is when something catches my eye. My upper arm is wrapped in cellophane. I vaguely remember going to a tattoo shop, and a blonde chick that had me sitting in a chair getting ready to push ink into my skin.

The pounding in my head is excruciating. One day I'll remember not to drink that much when I'm out with the guys. Today is obviously not that day. Reaching toward my nightstand, I fumble around the surface trying to find the bottle of Tylenol I used to keep there when I was in high school.

Then it hits me. I'm probably not going to find it. I'm sure Mom has moved all the little things around even though my room looks the same as it did last year. I am surprised, however, to find a shiny business card for a tattoo shop. Sitting up I examine the card.

Charleigh is written across the card in a swirly, cursive font. *That's* her name. Pieces are finally starting to fall into place. I remember Dylan suggesting tattoos, and Marshall wanting to talk us out of it. In the end we ended up at Life in Ink.

I'm pretty sure I was trying to flirt with Charleigh last night, but she wasn't a fan. The total look of disgust on her face when I told her to surprise me with the tattoo is etched in my memory. I don't know why she got so pissed. I gave her freedom to do whatever she wanted.

I look at my arm, eyeing the bandage warily. I'm not sure I want to see what she surprised me with, but there's no use putting it off. I did give her permission.

Unwrapping the cellophane, I envision the amazing tattoo I'll have. I took a peek at what she was sketching on the other side of that counter. She's amazing. I can't wait to see what she decided to give me.

The wrapping comes off easily and I blink a few times, not sure if what I'm seeing is actually there. No, she can't have put *that* on me. This has to be some sort of joke. I lick my finger and rub it over the ink now marring my skin.

Placing my feet on the floor, I stand up and walk to the bathroom that's connected to my room. I turn so that my arm is in the reflection in the mirror. I practically climb on the sink just to get a closer look. I'm never going to wear a sleeveless shirt again.

The tattoo isn't big, but it's enough that I didn't need

to get quite so close to the mirror. Staring back at me is Patrick from SpongeBob, eating a fucking pretzel. What is the point of the damn pretzel?

Stomping back to my nightstand, I grab the business card. The force curling the edges slightly. Where the hell is my phone? This girl is about to hear an earful.

I finally find it between my bed and nightstand when I hear a knock on the door. Grabbing the shirt I wore last night, I throw it over my head just in time for my bedroom door to open and my mother to walk in.

Most people would think the fact that she just walks into my room is weird, and it is, but she's been controlling for as long as I can remember. We don't have locks on our doors. Well, except for their room. They are the only ones allowed to have privacy.

In Mom's eyes, she should have access to everything I'm doing so that she can make sure I'm not getting into trouble. And, to make sure I'm not doing anything that will make her and Dad look like incompetent parents.

It was one of the reasons I liked hanging out at Tonya's house. Her parents are laid back and have a level of trust in her that I've never received from anyone.

"Why in the world are you just now getting out of bed, Jake," my mother practically shrieks.

"I was hanging out with the guys last night. We stayed out later than I thought." I have the good sense to look as innocent as possible without showing any hints of my hangover. That's something I've perfected over the years.

"Well," she huffs. "Don't let it happen again."

I roll my eyes. I can't help it. Does she think I'm twelve? "I won't, Mom."

I think she's done speaking so I turn to my bed to make it. Now that she knows I'm awake, there's no use trying to go back to sleep.

"We need you at dinner this evening." Her voice breaks the silence. "We are going to discuss how you're going to handle this whole Tonya debacle since you'll be home the entire summer."

The way she says handle makes it sound like I have no say in the matter. That whatever they've decided is what I'm going to do. I clench my fists and nod my head. I'll hear them out, but they are insane if they think they are going to dictate this area of my life. Especially when I'm not sure how I'm actually going to handle it all.

* * *

Marshall is sitting in a gaming chair. His room is an absolute mess, but at least it looks lived in. Our house is always immaculate. It looks staged for a photo shoot most of the time. Not as bad as Cami's house, the few times Tonya and I hung out there. But...close.

Randall and Dylan will be here soon, so if I want to talk to Marshall without feeling embarrassed, I better do it now.

"Hey man," I question. I mean for it to come out as a statement, but that isn't what happens.

Pressing pause on the football game he's playing, he turns the chair toward me. "I have a feeling you need to get something off your chest."

"You'd be right," I laugh.

"Shoot."

I rake my fingers through my hair. "My parents want me home for dinner to talk."

"That's normal, Dude. They are always in your business." He leans the chair back almost falling backward.

I nod because he's right. They are firm believers in always wanting to know what I'm doing. "They want to talk about Tonya and Layla. And, how to *handle* the situation." I wince internally. I hate the way Mom phrased it this morning.

Marshall's eyebrows rise. "What do they mean handle it? There's not really anything they can do."

He gives me a point stare, silently telling me there *is* something I can do, and that I need to talk to her. I want to explain. I want to tell him that I *can't*. If he saw how happy she was with Reaf over Spring Break, he'd never want to pop that bubble of happiness surrounding her. I didn't exactly make things easy for her when she was pregnant. If I'm being honest, I was a total douchebag. The fact that she gave me time to come to terms with having a daughter still baffles me.

Before I can say anything else, I hear hollering coming from the hallway. A few seconds later Randall and Dylan are barging through the doorway.

"What's up assholes?" Randall yells, slapping his hands on the wall.

There are days when I wonder why I'm friends with him. He's annoying on the best of days and fucking ridiculous on the worst.

"Not much," I lean against the headboard on

Marshall's bed. I don't have the patience to deal with these fools today, but I'm also eager to see their new tattoos without the wraps. The question is who is going to bring it up first. I don't have to wait long for the answer.

"I want to see everyone's tats," Dylan says, sitting on the edge of the bed.

Everyone else pulls their shirts off while I lift up my sleeve. The second they see mine, laughter fills the room.

"Why the hell did you get it on your arm?" Randall asks. "You realize it's going to be hard to cover that up during football season, right?"

I shrug. I don't know why I didn't have the artist put it in a different place, but I guess this was a part of her surprise. Ugh, I guess I'll be wearing t-shirts instead of tank tops under my uniform.

"Is that *Patrick*?" Dylan chuckles. "What is the point of him eating a pretzel?"

"Yeah, Man," Randall interjects. "Pretzels are the miracle whip of chips. Nobody likes them."

Marshall is still sitting in his gaming chair, though he's paused the game, shaking his head. I happen to know for a fact that he loves pretzels. His mom keeps the pantry stocked at all times when he's home.

I glance at my friends, trying to see if the tattoos they got match their personalities. Randall has some sort of tribal sun on his chest with thick lines. It's a stark contrast to his skin. He's not super pale, but he's not exactly tan either.

Dylan has a Celtic symbol on his back that looks

almost exactly like the symbol that Breaking Benjamin uses on their merchandise. It's pretty awesome and makes perfect sense. He's liked that band for as long as I can remember.

Marshall also has a tattoo on his chest. It's a compass. The design is simple, with a little bit of shading and the arrow pointing North. I wondered what he was going to get since he wasn't too keen on the idea of us getting tattoos, but this tattoo fits him perfectly. He's the steady one in our group. I don't think he realizes how much he equalizes all of us. Or, how much trouble he's probably kept us out of.

"I'm thinking I probably should have told my artist what I wanted," I sigh. "I was trying to flirt with her, but she's a feisty one."

"At least you didn't get stuck with the girl who had perpetual resting bitch face," Randall fires back.

Marshall blushes. That was the artist he had. I wonder what the reddening of his cheeks means, and before I have a chance to ask Dylan speaks up.

"Let's go out to the lake and hang out for a while."

Groaning, I get off the bed in search of my shoes. "I wish I could, but my parents are expecting me home for dinner."

"Can't you do it some other time?" Dylan asks.

A quick look at Marshall shaking his head means I need to get home and deal with whatever my parents are going to throw at me. "Afraid not."

I wave as I back out the door, "See y'all later. Let me know what the plan is for tomorrow."

I jog down the driveway and get in my car. I'm not ready for this dinner at all. I'm not even sure what I'm going to tell them if they question what I'm going to do about Layla.

charleigh

IT'S BEEN three days since that group of guys came in for ink. It's also been three days since I've done another tattoo. I've been cleaning the shop and taking appointments for everyone else. Does Uncle Corey not trust me? Did Bianca say something to him?

Maybe that Jake guy called and complained about the surprise tattoo I gave him. If that's the case, I'll gladly accept any consequences my uncle deems appropriate. That moron should have had an idea of what he wanted considering it's permanent. And...he could have maybe been a little less cocky.

I see guys like that come into the shop all the time. The ones who think they are invincible and can do whatever they want. But there's something about Jake in particular that I can't shake. Even though he was trying to be charming, keyword on trying, he seemed haunted. Like he lost a part of himself or doesn't know exactly what he wants.

That's the only reason I can come up with as to why

I'm thinking about him three days later. That's not normal for me. I date, but I don't get serious with anyone. My focus right now is to become a badass tattooist in the shop my uncle built from the ground up. We aren't overly famous like some of the shops in this area, but we're known for doing damn good work.

That's why entertaining any thoughts of some random guy is not a good idea. It would be a distraction from my goals. I've seen so many people throw away their wants for the person they *loved*, and I'm not doing that. I won't allow myself to be sidetracked. I quit college because it got in the way of earning my hours as an apprentice. Something I fear I'll always be if my uncle doesn't give me more clients.

I turn around, lean my back against the counter and study the shop. It's grown from what it used to be. My uncle was the only artist in here when he first opened it. I remember the weekends my parents would let me stay with Corey and Annie. The long nights when Annie would bring pizza by the shop because I wanted to spend my time here. I'm sure my mom wasn't thrilled with me spending all my time in a tattoo shop, but Dad couldn't deny that his brother is talented.

This is where my love of art began, and it's apparent with all my sketches my uncle has pinned to the wall in his work station. He's always fostered my talents, which is why I don't understand why he won't move me from apprentice to tattooist.

The bell on the door dings pulling me out of my thoughts. I know who it is before I turn around. I met this guy once, I should not be this aware of him.

I school my features, trying to come off as indifferent, but I don't think I pull it off. "Back for more surprise tattoos?"

"So, you remember me?" He smirks.

Ugh, why does that smirk cause butterflies to flutter in my stomach? I should be annoyed by his overabundance of confidence, but I'm not. This guy needs to get out of my life before I do something horrible...like *fall* for him.

I smile sweetly, "How could I forget? It's not often I ink Patrick or pretzels on anyone." Or, put ink on anyone at all. But, he doesn't need to know that.

Jake scrunches his eyebrows together, studying me. Maybe my smile came off as less sweet and more maniacal. That works, too. Maybe it'll warn him off from chasing me. If that's even what he's doing. I'm getting way ahead of myself.

That's when I notice the guy standing next to him, the level-headed sober one from the other night. His name starts with an M. Malcolm, Mark...

I look down at the counter where the appointment book is spread open. Oh, Marshall. That's his name. It's written in the three o'clock space next to Bianca's name in her loopy handwriting.

Frowning, I look at it again. I've been here all week and I haven't received any calls from him to schedule an appointment. That means he must have called Bianca directly. It's not technically against the rules, but Corey likes all the calls to come through the front desk so that he can keep up with what calls are coming in for each artist.

A throat clears, and I glance up. Marshall is standing really close to the counter now. "Is there a problem?"

"Uh, no." I shake my head. "I just didn't realize Bianca had any appointments before tonight."

Marshall's cheeks brighten to a nice shade of pink. "Yeah," he stammers. "She, um, gave me her phone number when we were here last time."

My mouth drops open. She doesn't do that, like *ever*. I wonder what it was about this guy, who is a lot younger than her, that peaked her interest.

"Okay, then," I reply. "You know where her station is. Nobody is in there right now, so go on back."

Jake doesn't follow his friend back toward the stations. Instead, he leans against the counter as if he has nothing better to do. There's no denying it. He's a good-looking guy. Lean and muscular from what I can see through the fabric of his shirt. Jeans sitting perfectly on his narrowed hips.

I casually lean to the left to get a view of his butt. I can't help it. I need to see if his ass is a nice as the rest of him. Just because he rubs me the wrong way doesn't mean I can't appreciate his physique. If I had to guess, I'd say this guy definitely plays sports.

Lifting my gaze to his face, his eyes on locked on me. One eyebrow lifted higher than the other in amusement. "Like something you see?"

I shrug. "Not really."

He jerks back in mock disbelief. His hand covering his chest like I've just wounded him. "Are you sure?"

"Yep," I reply, shuffling papers around. "Douchey jocks don't really do it for me."

"How did you know I play sports?"

"It was an educated guess. You have the build of an athlete." I don't know why I'm indulging him. He has "bad decision" written all over him. It may as well be inked across his forehead. Come to think of it, that could be my next surprise tattoo for him.

No, not *next*. I don't need him coming in the shop after this anymore. I look through the appointment book to see who has a client coming in soon. "Shouldn't you be back there with your friend? For moral support or whatever?"

jake

I STARE in awe at the art plastered on the walls. There's a little bit of everything from dragons to skulls, and even a few fairies. Whoever drew them is crazy talented, and I can't image ever being that good at something. I'm going to school on a football scholarship, but I don't know what I'm going to do past that. I haven't thought that far ahead even though I should.

Scanning the various scenes before me I wonder if Charleigh is responsible for any of them. I had every intention of calling her a few days ago to give her a piece of my mind. I'm still not happy about the tattoo, but I wasn't exactly an easy client. Come to think of it, I should probably work on that being an asshole thing.

I can't stop thinking about the feisty blonde. She doesn't even look like the type of person who would have any tattoos, let alone work in a shop. She doesn't wear the tight dresses or dramatic makeup like the female tattoo artists on those reality shows. I guess what people say is true...looks can be deceiving. But the light in her eyes when she was drawing the night we came in tells me this is her passion.

A throat clearing behind me makes me jump. I whirl around to see an older man standing at the counter Charleigh vacated. He looks vaguely familiar. Was he here the other night?

"Is there anything I can help you with?"

When the hell did this guy even come in? I didn't hear him at all. His tall, muscular, and has tattoos covering what I can see of his arms. He's intimidating, standing with his arms crossed, and I have a gut feeling he's trying to be.

"No, sir," I reply. "My buddy is in there with Bianca, and I'm out here admiring your artwork."

I shift my weight, suddenly unable to stand still under this man's scrutiny. I remember who he is now. Charleigh called him Corey, and I'm pretty sure they are family. He looks old enough to be her father, but I don't think that's right.

"They aren't all mine," he says. "Some of them belong to my niece."

So, I was right. Family, and the way he's staring at me, eyes hard, tells me he'll do anything for her.

"You mean Charleigh?" I ask, trying to come off as nonchalant. I must be failing at it because he smirks.

"Yep, that's her."

"Why isn't she tattooing today?"

I see his shoulders sag just the tiniest bit. "She has other things she has to do around the shop."

I nod because I don't know what else to say. At just that moment Marshall comes out of the room Bianca works in and saves me from trying to make small talk with this guy that would definitely not approve of me thinking about his niece.

"Ready to go?" Marshall asks through the stupid grin on his face. I need to drag information out of him later because he's never had the puppy love look he's wearing right now. Not even when he dated girls in high school.

"Yes," I respond a little too quickly. Corey makes me nervous, and I need to talk to him anyway. He didn't leave me much room to talk on the way here. He kept going on and on about the work he wanted added to the compass he got last time. But, I need his advice because my parents are insane.

I push open the door and a gust of hot air immediately engulfs me. It definitely feels like summer in Texas. I should be used to it by now, but it's always shocking after leaving an airconditioned building. I can feel the sweat forming on my chest. It's not even June, and the temperature is already enough to make people want to hide indoors.

Before I can put one foot in the direction of the truck, Marshall speaks up. "You want to grab a bite to eat while we're here? I haven't eaten anything since breakfast and I'm starving."

I'm about tell him no but think better of it. If we go back to his house there's a chance Dylan and Randall will show up, and I won't get my chance to talk to him. "Sure, I could eat."

There's a restaurant across the street that looks promising. We wait at the light until it's okay for us to cross the street. I definitely don't want to get run-over by someone paying more attention to their phone than they are the road.

Rock music is spilling from the speakers when we walk in. There's no podium for us to wait at to be seated so we find a booth that isn't near anyone. I don't want anyone to hear our conversation.

We've barely had time to look over the menu when a waitress approaches the table. "What can I get for ya?"

"Can I get a sweet tea?" I ask. There's nothing better on a hot day than a glass of sweet iced tea.

I'm not sure what Marshall gets to drink. I'm looking over the menu, trying to figure out if I really want to talk about this.

"Hey man, what's up with you?" Marshall questions. "You're studying that menu like you're going to have a test."

When I look up I notice our drinks are already sitting on the table. I didn't even notice the waitress come back. Marsh must have asked for more time for us to look at the menu.

"A lot," I reply. "This crap with Tonya and my parents is going to drive me insane."

He places his arms on the table and leans forward. "I was wondering when you were going to bring dinner with your parents up. You pretty much went silent on everyone for the past couple of days."

"Sorry about that," I shrug. "I just needed to wrap my head around what my parents suggested, and it still seems ludicrous."

Before I can continue, our waitress is back. "Do you know what you want to eat?"

Both of us order a burger and fries. It's pretty impossible to screw that up, and since this isn't a fast food place it will take a bit for our food to be ready.

"Let me guess," Marshall starts. "They want you to give up your rights to Layla."

I don't miss that he says it as a statement. "How did you know that?" I ask, heavy on the sarcasm.

"Because your parents are insane and only think about appearances?" He rolls his eyes. "You can't tell me that you didn't have any idea they would want you to do that."

I begin tearing the corner of the napkin serving as a placemat for my tea. "You're right. I guessed that would be part of it." I pause. "But they took it a step further."

"I can't wait to hear what bullshit they suggested."

"It's definitely shit, that's for sure."

He leans in even closer, "Which is?"

I sigh, shoulders sagging, defeat in my voice. "They want to basically give her a big enough amount of money to say that the baby isn't mine."

Marshall jerks back so hard he nearly knocks his drink over causing the few people in the restaurant to glance our direction.

"Are you fucking kidding me?" His eyes are wide, mouth hanging open, shocked and in disbelief. "They actually suggested that? You aren't going to agree to it, are you?"

"Hell no," my voice rises, bring more eyes to our table. "Why would you even think I could do that?"

Our food arrives at precisely that moment. Our waitress, Ginger, according to the name tag I'm just now noticing, slides two baskets holding our burgers onto the table. "Is there anything else I can get y'all?"

I wave my hand, "No, we're good."

"All right, if you need anything just let me know." She winks at me before walking back toward the bar on the other side of the room.

What in the world was up with the winking? She has to know that I'm way too young for her. I take a bite of my burger, and nearly groan because it is that good. It's not too well done, and the condiments don't overpower the taste.

I set the burger back in the basket and pick up a fry. "I know I screwed things up with Tonya, and she was a saint when I asked for time, but I couldn't do that to her. Or Layla."

"Have you talked to her since dinner with the idiots you call parents?"

"No, not yet. But I'm going to."

"Dude," Marshall says with every ounce of authority he can muster. He's the only one that can get away with using that tone with me. "You *need* to talk to her." He dips a fry into the pile of ketchup he's poured on a napkin. "Before your mom gets it in her head to take matters into her own hands."

I throw my hands up. In anger or aggravation? I don't know. But now that he's put that thought in my head, I wouldn't put it past my mother to show up at Tonya's house with her checkbook in hand.

"I will...tomorrow," I say. I just hope she'll hear me out. And, if I'm lucky, Reaf won't be there.

charleigh

VISITING my parents is different than when I was living here. They make more of an effort when I come over, and it's weird. The table in the dining room is set with perfection. Place settings in front of three of the four chairs surrounding the table. When I still lived here, the plates were stacked next to the stove, so we could serve ourselves in the kitchen and then bring our food to the table.

There are bowls and platters shoved together in the middle of the table. I glance over them trying to see what they've cooked up tonight. Some of my favorite foods, red potatoes, corn on the cob, and grilled pork chops fill the space. I have a feeling they want to have a serious talk tonight. Even though I doubt I'll want to hear what they say, I'll suffer through it because I never eat as well at home as I do here.

Mom walks into the dining room, carrying a bowl filled to the brim with salad. She even added bell peppers and bits of bacon to it. "Hi, honey. You're here early."

"Yep," I swipe a pepper from the salad before she sets it down. "Uncle Corey let me leave before my shift was up because we were slow."

"Well," she replies. "That's nice of him."

I know she loves Corey, but she doesn't agree with him helping me fulfill my dreams. I think deep down she blames him for my love of tattoos. Even if I hadn't spent my time at the shop as a child, I think I still would have loved them.

"Mh-hm," I mumble, and quickly change the subject. "How have you and Dad been?"

She smiles with a little twinkle in her eye. I know they miss having me home, but I also know they are enjoying every second of being empty nesters. "Great." She says. "My garden is finally starting to produce some vegetables. I actually have some to send home with you."

"That's awesome," I exclaim. "Though, I don't know why you worry. You've always been able to grow anything."

She shrugs. "True, but it seems like summer is starting earlier every year and it ends up killing off my plants."

It's the price of living in Texas. I've never lived anywhere else, but geez...the weather could be a little more consistent.

"Where's Dad?" I ask. "He's usually in here as soon as the food is on the table."

"He's cleaning off the grill," she rolls her eyes. "He is obsessed with keeping that thing clean."

"Ah." I shouldn't be surprised. "Speaking of the

devil." I point toward Dad just walked in from the backyard.

"Only good things, I hope." He walks straight toward me and wraps me up in a hug. "How are you, sweetheart?"

"I'm good." I murmur into his shoulder, trying not to grimace at the slight dampness of his shirt from sweat.

I pull back and take a look at him. He seems more at ease than I've ever seen him. Alone time seems to be doing him and Mom some good.

"Can we eat now?" I ask. "Smelling all this food is making me hungry."

Dad goes around and pulls Mom's chair out for her. Chivalry isn't dead. At least, not in this household. Seeing them still very much in love gives me hope that one day, when I'm ready, I'll have someone to do the same things for me.

We pile food on our plates and I don't even wait to dig in. The potatoes are the first thing on my agenda. I take a bit and nearly moan. They are soft but slightly crisp all at the same time. I taste a hint of basil. "Wow, Mom. These are really good."

She grins, "Thanks. I've been on the computer looking for recipes." I can tell she's really excited about this. "I got this one from The Pioneer Woman."

"It's definitely a winner," I shovel more in my mouth. "I want these every day."

I've already cleared half my plate when I see Mom not so subtly signaling Dad. Uh oh, I guess they figure now is the time to harp on me for whatever reason.

"Charleigh," Dad begins, waiting for me to look up.

"Your mom and I have been talking. And, while we fully support you following your dream at the tattoo shop, we really think you should go back to school."

They haven't brought this up in a long time. Why now? I've finally done my first tattoo, and hope I'll be doing more soon.

"I can't do both," I respond. "I told y'all that when I decided to take this path. It was too hard trying to get in all my hours as an apprentice and keep up with my schoolwork."

"We know, honey," Mom interjects. "But, it's been two years and you still aren't doing any tattoos." Sighing, she continues. "We just don't want you to keep down this road if it isn't going to be a lucrative career for you."

"That's not true," I argue. "I did a tattoo last weekend."

"That's one in two years, Charleigh," Mom says feeling like she's made a point.

"But, I *know* Uncle Corey is going to give me more clients. I can feel it in my gut." I hear the whine creep into my voice, and I don't want to sound like a bratty child. But...this is my dream. This is what I've worked so hard for the past couple of years. "It just takes time, like any other trade."

Dad nods accepting the last part of my argument, at least. He steps in before Mom and I get into a fight about it again. "At least think about it."

I nod. There's nothing else I can do. I don't want to disappoint them, but I'm not giving up who I am or what I want to appease them.

* * *

The rest of dinner and dessert went well. We talked about the ridiculous tattoo I gave Jake. Dad thought it was pretty hysterical. I'm happy he found the humor in it. Mom thought it was mean. Eh, he should have known what he wanted and not taken permanently inking something into his skin as a joke.

Now, though I'm sprawled across the sofa in my tiny apartment watching reruns of *Project Runway*. I have no desire to be any sort of fashionista, but I love seeing what they come up. Even if the designers make something I would never in a million years wear, I applaud them for their creativity and confidence in their design.

I also let the conversation with my parents run through my head. While going to back to school would be hard, it's not impossible. The shop doesn't open until two in the afternoon, and during the week we close at ten. That would give me time to take at least some online classes. Who knows, maybe I could go to school for marketing. It would definitely help with finding clients for myself, as well as bring in more customers for the shop.

Even though Life in Ink has been around for decades, we don't get the traffic that some of the newer, flashier shops receive. I want to do more to contribute to the place that is giving me a shot, and this may be the way to do that.

I still have time to make a decision. The Fall semester doesn't start for another two months, I'll decide by then.

The last thing I remember before my eyes close and I drift off to sleep is a skirt that I would totally wear made completely out of polaroid photos.

jake

I WOKE up this morning with a text from Marshall. It said two words...*Go NOW*.

If he were here right now, he'd be pushing my ass out of this bed. I wouldn't blame him, either. I need to talk to Tonya. I have to know if she will still allow me to be a part of Layla's life even though I've been absent for the past three months.

I roll out of bed and make my way to the bathroom. I've never been more grateful than I am right now for the bathroom being attached to my room. If I were to walk out and either one of my parents see the dread and confusion written all over my face, they would no doubt question me until I told them what was going on.

I step into the shower with every intention of it being quick so I can face the consequences of my decisions, but I don't get out until the water cools. Drying off, I look in the mirror. When did I become the guy that runs from his problems? When did I start doing everything my parents told me without question?

I remember being a child that tested his parents' patience. But somewhere around junior high I started taking their advice and rules as some sort of golden standard. They also informed me at that age that I was to do what they say, or they would no longer support me. That seems like a pretty brutal threat to most, but I knew it was for my own good. Especially if I wanted to see the level of success they had and wanted the same lifestyle they have. I didn't question any of it.

The only person I know that has been raised the same way I have is Cami. But she fought the rules her dad placed on her at every turn. We've also never been able to stand each other, so I couldn't go to her at any point in mine and Tonya's relationship.

I'm stalling. I know I am, but I can't seem to get into any hurry to go talk to the mother of my child. I brush my teeth and get dressed. As much as I wish this whole situation was different, I need to go *now* before I lose my nerve.

Throwing my dirty clothes in the hamper, I crack the door open. Listening for any sound of life. There's nothing. Mom and Dad are still asleep or already out for the day.

Tiptoeing down the hall and stairs, I grab my keys from the line of hooks by the front door. I lock up the house and head to my car. I should give her some warning that I'm coming over, but then she'll have time to prepare her speech to turn down any sort of relationship I want to have with Layla, and I can't let that happen.

I just hope Reaf isn't there. While I know that things

between Tonya and I are over, him being the father figure in Layla's life still rankles me. I don't know that I will ever get over him being there for her when I had my head up my ass, but it's just one more thing that I'm not fully capable of handling right now.

* * *

My palms are sweating. I'm sitting in my car across the street from Tonya's house. To others I may look like a possible stalker or creeper, but I'm just trying to gather my wits and composure. I'm not sure what is going to happen within those walls, but I hope we can come to some sort of compromise.

I step out of my car, and gently close the door. Looking both ways before I cross the street, I wipe the palms of my hands on my shorts. I don't want to appear as nervous as I feel. I knock on the door and await the surprised reaction I'm likely to get.

I'm shocked when Cami opens the door. "What do *you* want?"

"Wh-what are you doing here?" I stammer. I shouldn't be the least bit surprised since she's always here. But I am because it's early, and she's normally still asleep.

"Opening the door, dumbass," she replies with an eye roll.

"Obviously," I snort. "But you're not usually joining the land of the living until around lunch."

"Well, I'm living here for the summer." Cami leans against the door, barring my entrance. "Not that it's any of your business. And, I'm running late for work, so I hope you aren't blocking me in."

"I'm parked across the street, so you don't have to worry about that."

Before she continues on her way out the door, I stop her. "Can you let Tonya know I'm here?"

Another eye roll is directed at me. "I guess. But I'm warning you…if you upset her, I will destroy you."

I definitely don't miss her stunning personality. I don't know what I ever did to her to make her hate me so much, but I'm relieved that I don't have to see her on a day to day basis anymore.

"Thanks," I mutter into thin air.

Less than a minute later, Cami breezes past me bumping into my shoulder on the way to her car. As much as she annoys me, I admire her ability to not care what people say or think.

Tonya is making her way toward the front door and all my annoyance is replaced with nervousness. The last time I was here I made an ass of myself, and I'm hoping today isn't a repeat of that spectacular performance.

"Hi, Jake," she takes Cami's spot leaning against the door. She's trying to appear relaxed, but her back is ramrod straight, and I can practically feel the apprehension coming off her in waves.

I pull my shirt away from my chest, trying to keep it from sticking to my skin in the early morning heat.

"Can we, um, talk?" I ask, shoving my hands into my pockets.

"Sure," she swings her arm to her side, allowing my entrance.

"Where's Layla?"

"She's taking her morning nap. She's been up since about six this morning." She yawns, and I feel bad for barging in unannounced. I should have let her know I was coming.

I take a seat in the recliner. I don't miss the fact that she's sitting on the sofa as far away from me as possible. Her legs curled under her, waiting to see what I'm here to say.

Looking around the living room, trying to kill time, I notice it's still pretty much the same. The only difference being the baby toys and pacifiers strewn throughout.

I pick up the pacifier sitting on the coffee table, playing with the small handle to give my hands something to do before I look up at her. "I'm not going to beat around the bush." I pause, "I want to be in Layla's life."

Tonya scoffs. "Are you sure? Because the last time I saw you, you were speeding off down the road when I was trying to talk to you."

My shoulders sag. I wish I could take the blanket settled on the back of the recliner and hide beneath it. That's preferable than trying to validate my actions. Especially, when I can't.

"I know, and I'm sorry." I set the pacifier back on the table. "I freaked out. I knew I would see you and Reaf while I was home for Spring Break. But then...then I saw him pick up Layla, and I got mad. I had no right to get angry, but I was just the same. I didn't want to do anything to ruin your day, so I did the only thing I could. I left."

Tonya pinches the bridge of her nose and sighs. "I

can respect the fact that you know you were in the wrong. But, Reaf is going to be a major part of Layla's life. He's the one that's been here and been supportive. Hell, he's even changed her dirty diapers."

I'm about to argue. She chose him instead of me. The words are on the tip of my tongue. I don't say them, though. Being a jealous asshole isn't going to win me any favors. And, honestly, she was right to not take me back. I wasn't ready to be the man she needed, and we are totally different people.

"I know. And, I'll work on my jealousy." I clasp my hands together to keep them from balling into fists. "I just want to be a part of Layla's life. I want her to know that even though I screwed up for the first few months of her life, I don't regret her."

A tiny cry comes from a speaker beside Tonya. I didn't realize she had anything beside her. "Sounds like sleeping beauty has woken up."

Tonya stands to go check on our daughter. "Can I... can I see her?"

Tonya nods. "She's probably in a grouchy mood. Even though she wakes up at the crack of dawn, she is not a morning person."

She leads me into what used to be the spare bedroom, and it's been completely transformed. Instead of the beige walls with white trim, there's a solid bright yellow wall. The others are painted an off-white color, and princess signs hang all over the room.

"Wow," I say. "That's a lot of pink and yellow."

Tonya shrugs. "It started out just yellow. The rest just kind of exploded after we found out Little Bean was a girl." She crosses the room, pulling out a diaper and container of wipes, setting them on a table that has a pad on top of it.

I take that time to peek over the edge of the crib. Layla is lying there, fists curled, small cries spilling from her lips. She has on a onesie that says, "Future Bush Fan." I roll my eyes, only Tonya would force her love of Gavin Rossdale on our child.

"She's not going to bite you, you know?" Tonya says. "She literally can't because she doesn't have any teeth. Go ahead and pick her up."

I laugh. I mean she obviously can't bite me. I'm not a moron. But the thought of picking up a tiny human is terrifying. What if I do it wrong, or drop her?

I reach into the crib and place my hands under arms before lifting her to my chest. Tonya moves one of my hands to just under her neck. "This will help stabilize the upper part of her body a bit."

She's not wrong. Even though it appears Layla has some control of her head, she's squirmy. I move her close to me and bounce walk across the room to the table. Tonya slides her out of my arms and makes quick work of changing her diaper.

I'm in awe. Number one because for such a little person she has a foul-smelling diaper. But also, because Tonya handles her with such surety, like she's had years of practice instead of three months.

She disposes of the diaper, then holds Layla in my direction. I quickly take her. Pulling her to me once again. My heart has never felt as full as it does in this moment. This is the first time I'm seeing my daughter, but already she has me wrapped around her finger.

Settling into the rocking chair in the corner of the room, I place Layla in my lap. "Hi, Baby Girl. I'm your daddy."

I know she can't respond, but the huge, toothless smile that takes over is answer enough. There's nothing that can bring me down from this moment.

I'm lounging on Marshall's couch flipping through many pictures I took of Layla, pausing on the one I had Tonya snap of the two of us. I can see how proud I am of this little person. I toss the phone to Marshall so he can see her.

"I'm glad you finally manned up and talked to Tonya," he says scrolling through the pictures.

"Me too. Thank you for giving me the push I needed."

"I take it everything went okay?" He asks.

"Yep. We're going to arrange a day in the park soon."

Marshall laughs, "I sense a but coming on."

"Reaf is going to be there," I grimace. "But I guess if we're going to attempt to co-parent, I need to deal with him being around. He's been good to her while I've been trying to figure my shit out."

"Look at you being an adult."

I yank my phone out of his hand. "Don't be an asshole."

"Alright, I'll quit." He stands and picks up two

controllers from the coffee table. "Want to throw down on some 2K?"

I don't reply. I grab the offered controller and try my best to beat him. With the way I'm feeling right now, even a loss in a video game won't bring me down.

charleigh

IT'S BEEN over two weeks since I tattooed Jake, and I have yet to put ink on another person. It's really starting to frustrate me. I know Corey approves of the sketches I've been doing. He's finding less and less to criticize when I show him. It's part of the reason I'm so annoyed with the whole situation.

It's also why I'm mopping the floor like it's personally offended me. Maybe I should let some of my anger and frustration follow me home. There's no telling how spotless it would be if I scrubbed like I am right now.

I hear footsteps approaching from behind. "You know that's all you're going to be, right?"

Ugh, why does Bianca have to choose this moment to come in here and be bitchy. That's one thing I can't take right now.

"Why does my place in this shop matter so much to you? It's not like you'll be out of a job when I come on board." I slam the mop into the water bucket.

"I just wanted to let you know that if you haven't

made it by now, you most likely never will." She turns on her heel and walks back into her workroom. Not even giving me the chance to reply.

I really wish I understood what her problem with me is. She's someone I've looked up to since she started working at Life in Ink. I've watched her work with precision and professionalism, but she takes every opportunity to put me down. I'm beginning to question whether I even have what it takes to pursue this dream of mine.

I continue mopping because the shop is practically a ghost town this afternoon. I have a feeling it will pick up this evening, but for now this is keeping me busy. I'm trying to let my mind wander, but it's not working. I'm still stuck on the fact that my uncle is holding me back, and I want to know why.

The bell about the door dings, so I set the mop aside preparing to see who's come in, but I'm met by Corey in the hallway. He's carrying a bag of food.

He lifts it in my direction. "Want to take a break and have lunch with your favorite uncle?"

I roll my eyes, little does he know he's not my favorite anything right now. "Sure."

Putting away the mop and bucket, I try to figure out how I'm going to talk to Corey about my place in the shop. I need to know if I'm wasting my time. If everything that I've been working toward is for nothing.

When I walk into his office, he's setting food on his desk. I notice he made a special trip for me to get pasta. He must have sensed my mood before he left to get lunch.

"Sit down, Charleigh. Whatever you were doing can

wait." Corey says before taking a seat behind the old metal desk he's had for as long as I can remember.

"Can I ask you something?" I say before taking a seat across from him.

"Sure." He pauses, "you know you can come to me with anything."

I take a deep breath, trying to find the words I want to say without offending him. But end up blurting out, "Why haven't you let me tattoo anyone else?"

I expected to see some sort of surprise on his face, but I guess he could see it coming. "I was wondering when you would ask again."

"Then why not just come out and say something. My drawings have gotten better. I'm ready for this. I feel like I've been ready for a while."

"This is what I was waiting for, Charleigh." He sets his burger down. "I wanted you to come to me and demand answers. I wanted you to show me that you had the confidence."

I put my fork down and lean back in the chair. No fucking way. He mind tricked me. "Seriously, that's why you haven't let me claim my workspace? Because I didn't confront you sooner?"

He nods. "That's exactly it. I needed to know that you wanted it. That you wouldn't settle for just cleaning the shop."

"That's actually a relief." I pick up my fork again. "I was beginning to think my mother put you up to not letting me take my place in the shop."

He cringes. "Actually...she approached me about that very thing."

Nearly choking on my spaghetti, I gasp. "And you *listened* to her."

"Hell no," he laughs. "I've never let your aunt push me around. Do you honestly think I'd let your mother tell me what to do in my own shop?"

"You're right." I take another bite. "I'm glad you didn't give in. That may have ruined you being my favorite uncle."

We finish the rest of our lunch in companionable silence. That's what I love about him. We can talk and goof around, but we can also just enjoy each other's company. This is how I know I can work with him.

* * *

I'm putting up the last of the cleaning supplies. Even though Corey said I can start tattooing, there are still things that have to be done around the shop. I'm no longer angry cleaning the place. The windows are now clean, and I've restocked everyone's workspace.

I walk across the shop and toward the room where I'll be working. Visions of how I'm going to decorate it dance through my head. I'm not sure if I want to go dark and broody, or the complete opposite and keep it light and fun. Bianca walks across the shop, and I automatically scratch off the whole broody feel. I'd rather it feel more like me anyway. A lot of turquoise, grays, and black. All of my favorite colors. People aren't going to know what to expect when they enter my area.

Heading to the counter to see what sketches I have to hang up in my area, I'm stopped dead in my tracks when the door opens. The little ding announcing a new visitor. Jake is standing in the doorway, looking around the shop until his eyes land on me.

He's not with any of his friends, and I'm curious as to why he's here.

jake

I STOP RIGHT after walking into the shop. Charleigh looks like a deer caught in the headlights. Mouth gaping open and eyes as wide as saucers. Even in this moment of surprise she is beautiful. Her long blonde hair is piled on top of her head in some sort of bun. She also looks lighter, like a weight has been lifted off her shoulders.

"Jake," she finally shakes off the shock. "What are you doing here?"

Shoving my hands in my pockets, I shift on my feet. "I, um, actually came to talk to you."

Coming here seemed like a great idea when I was making the thirty-minute drive to Dallas. Now...I feel like a moron for even thinking she'd be willing to talk to me after our interactions the previous two times. But I want this done right, and I've seen her work.

"Oh yeah?" Charleigh places her arms on the counter and leans forward. "What could you possibly want to talk to me about?"

There's a teasing in her voice that I haven't heard before. I almost wonder if she's been abducted by aliens or replaced with a changeling. Both would be more believable than our interaction right now.

"We-well," I stutter. Jesus, I can't even talk around her. "I want you to design a tattoo for me. I'm not sure what, yet. But I know you have amazing skills."

"Are you sure you don't want another surprise tattoo?" She questions.

"Definitely," I smile. "I don't need to wake up one morning with SpongeBob tattooed across my forehead."

Charleigh shakes her head and looks down, hiding her smile. "Pity."

I'm sure she's just itching to give me another absurd tattoo. I can practically see cartoon images flit across her eyes.

I walk closer to the counter, "So, can you do it?"

"I can," she drawls. She's flipping through the appointment book, barely paying any attention to me. "But the more accurate question is *will* I."

Inwardly groaning, I sigh. "Charleigh, will you design a tattoo for me?"

She snaps the appointment book closed causing me to jump. That small book should not put off that level of sound. "I'll think about it."

"That's it? You'll think about it?"

"Yep," she smiles. I don't think I've ever seen anyone with a smile like hers. It lights up the entire room. I mean, the room was already bright before since they don't seem to have any curtains covering their windows. But the way she beams adds an extra sparkle.

"Um, okay," I respond. I'm not ready to leave yet, so I stroll around the room hoping to see new art plastered on the walls. Wondering if I will be able to pick out the ones that Charleigh has contributed to this unique canvas.

I feel Charleigh's presence behind me. It'd be hard not to notice her. I feel like everything, aside from my parents, in my life is starting to align. It gives me the courage to ask Charleigh the other thing I came here for.

She's been on my mind since the last time I came with Marshall. I want to know what makes her tick, what makes her love art the way she so obviously does, and what her fears are. I have a feeling it will be harder to uncover more than anything else.

Finally, I walk back to the counter, where she is still standing trying to hide the fact that she watched my every move as I made my way around the shop. I want to get this done before her uncle makes an appearance. I definitely don't want to ask her out with him standing over me.

"Is there something else you needed?" Charleigh asks.

"Actually," I wait until she looks me in the eye. "How would you like to go out on a date?"

She jerks back. "You can't be serious. We barely even know each other." Slipping her sketch book open, she takes a pencil and starts drawing. "Besides, I don't think it would be a very good idea, and I'm much too busy to date anyone."

I glance over the counter trying to see what she's

working on. "That's kind of the whole point of a date...to get to know each other."

"Thanks, I'll pass," she deadpans.

I grab the pencil out of her hand and grab one of the business cards off the counter. I jot down my number and hand both the pencil and card to her. "You can't spend every waking hour in this shop. Live a little. What have you got to lose?"

Not giving her a chance to reply I walk toward the door. Just before opening it, I turn toward her and call out, "If you change your mind text me." And I leave. The ball's in her court, now.

When I get to my car I throw my hand up in the air like that guy in that eighties movie Tonya made me watch when we were dating. I still have it. I thought all my charm and will died when I realized that Tonya no longer wanted me. Hell, it definitely felt like it because I couldn't get a date at all.

I'm expecting my phone to sound with an alert at any moment. But, it doesn't. My excitement dulls, but only just a little. I'll find any reason I can to go to Life in Ink until Charleigh gives me a chance.

The drive home takes twice as long. Apparently everyone in Dallas decided to be on the highways at the very moment I needed to go home. I will never understand why this area is always so backed up. It doesn't matter what time of day it is, there are always brake lights but nothing to really cause them.

Country music is blaring through my radio as I make my way toward Ashville. Charleigh may not have text me yet, but I know in my gut she will. She wouldn't have been flirting with me earlier otherwise.

I almost call the guys to see what they are up to but decide to go home instead. Walking through the door, though, I wish I would have gone anywhere else. The words being slung from my parents makes it sound like a warzone has taken over our living room.

"What do you mean he hasn't taken care of it yet," my father yells.

"As far as I know he hasn't even tried to contact Tonya. So, that's something you'll have to take up with him." My mother shrieks.

I softly close the door, trying not to make a sound. I have no doubt they are talking about me. And I don't feel like listening to their shit.

I try to sneak past the opening to get to the stairs, but my dad must catch the movement out of the corner of his eyes. "Jake, get in here," he bellows.

My shoulders sag. So much for avoiding this. "Yes, sir."

"Have you talked to Tonya, yet?"

"No, sir." The best way to get this over with quickly is by showing the most respect I can, even though he doesn't deserve it.

"Why the hell not?" he demands.

"I haven't had the chance, sir."

"You don't have a job, and all you do is hang out with the idiots you went to school with. Don't give me the bullshit that you haven't had time."

"Sorry, sir. I'll take care of it this week." I lie through my teeth. I have no intentions in following through with their ridiculous plan.

"You better," he says. "Don't forget, everything you have, we've given you. We can take it all away, and let you struggle."

"I understand." I say and turn around taking the stairs two at a time so I won't have to be in their presence any longer.

I don't know why they think they can just buy people off. I know they aren't hurting for money, but this affects more than just my life. And I'm not going to give up any claim on my daughter.

Closing the door to my room, I pull out my phone. I need to put a lock code on here before they get any ideas and start snooping through my phone to see what contact I've had with Tonya.

I've just set the passcode, and as I'm reaching toward the button to put it on the lock screen, a message pops up. It's from a number I don't know.

Unknown number: Yes

Me: Is this Charleigh

Unknown number: Do you hand out your number to a lot of girls?

Me: I knew you would change your mind.

Unknown number: don't get cocky...

. . .

I quickly add her contact information to the number. Even though I'm still pissed at my parents, that one three letter word made my night slightly better. Now, it's time to plan a date that will sweep her off her feet.

charleigh

THIS APARTMENT IS NOT big enough for the amount of pacing I'm doing. I lost count of how many times I've gone from one wall to the other. I'm starting to regret saying yes to Jake. I'm not even a hundred percent sure why I did. Maybe it was all the happy endorphins from being told I can start taking clients, who knows.

I've never been so nervous or apprehensive about a date. I should not have butterflies caused by a guy that I don't even really know. The few times I've been around him all he's done is annoy me...on *purpose*. I mean, who does that?

I don't even know what we're doing. When I asked him what I needed to wear, he just replied back with *something comfortable*. Comfortable to me is a band t-shirt and yoga pants, but sure he doesn't mean that sort of comfortable.

I'm almost tempted to text Bianca and ask her if what I'm wearing is okay, just so I have another female's perspective. **I quickly decide against that. Besides**

being super humiliating, it's just one more thing for her to give me shit about.

I stop at the full length mirror hanging on the wall, first looking at all my sketches surrounding it, then studying myself. I have on light blue skinny jeans that hug the few curves I have just right. I paired them with a solid white tee, covered up by a plaid long sleeve shirt tied at the waist. I have no idea if where we are going is to be indoors and cold, or outside and hot. I finished the look off with my Vans. I'm tempted to switch them out for wedges but decide against it.

Running my fingers through my long, wavy hair, I make sure my makeup isn't smeared after all my move-ment. I grab a hair tie and shove it in my small bag just in case I want to throw my hair into a ponytail later. Let's be honest, it's more than likely going to happen. I love my long hair, but it usually just gets in my way.

I'm starting to sit on the sofa so I don't wear a hole in my floor with all the pacing when there's a knock at the door. I jump. I knew he would eventually be here, but I still jump. The sound of his knuckles on the wood door scaring the hell out of me. I look at my phone. He's early. Not by much but still. I figured he would be the type of guy that is always late.

I start speed walking to the door, my nerves pushing me forward. I pause, willing my feet to move at a normal pace. I continue to the door. Hands shaking as I grip the knob. I take a deep breath, let it out slowly, and open the door.

His hand is raised mid-air, as if he was about to knock again. He jerks back in surprise when it registers that the door is in fact already open. "I wasn't sure you were going to answer."

"I just had to put a few things in my bag," I lie. He doesn't have to know that I'm completely freaking out. I've been on dates before. But, not with anyone that has intrigued me, or driven me as crazy, as he does.

He takes a second to look me over. Starting at my feet and working his way up, until his eyes land on mine. "You look amazing," he barely whispers.

He grabs a piece of hair that has fallen in my face, gently pushing it behind my ear. "I'm surprised your hair is down." His hand is hovering by my cheek. He quickly moves it to his side. "I like it like this."

I blush. There's no doubt my cheeks are tinged pink against my pale skin. I also can't help the small grin forming on my lips. I'm so used to being around everyone at the shop. They've treated me like one of the guys for as long as I can remember. It's nice to be treated with fragility sometimes. It's a great reminder that I can be more than just one thing.

I'm not sure how to react without completely ruining the moment. "Are you ready to go?" I blurt out, rocking on my heels. Any chances of appearing like I'm not nervous are now completely blown out of the water.

"Yep," he says. "Are you?"

"Well, I did ask," I reply. "Let me grab my bag and lock up."

He waits patiently at the door, not even trying to come into my space without being invited. Maybe he's actually a gentleman, and not the cocky athlete that walked into the tattoo shop. I'm not getting my hopes up, but we'll see how tonight goes.

He steps back as I close the door, allowing me my space. Reaching his hand out, he looks me in the eye, silently asking for permission to take my hand. I place my hand in his, and we make our way down the stairs in silence. It's not weird or awkward, either. There just isn't a need to fill the void with words. I do wonder who is going to break the silence first.

Leaving my building, we stop short at a black truck in pristine condition. He presses a button on his key fob to unlock the doors, opens the door for me, and gives me a hand to get into his lifted truck. It's a good thing he did, or I might have scrambled in ungracefully.

He walks around the front of the truck and slides into his seat with ease before starting the truck. "I have two questions for you."

He takes a moment to check the road before pulling out into traffic. "You can ask, but I might not answer."

I roll my eyes. The cockiness is still there. "First, how did you manage to find parking right in front of my building?" I take a breath. "Second, how in the hell did you fit this behemoth in that spot?"

Laughter fills the cab of the truck. "We're going on our first date, and those are the hard pressing questions you have for me?"

"Um, yeah." I fiddle with the strap of my bag. "Also, where are we going?"

"That's three questions, Charleigh."

"Humor me."

He settles his arm on the console between us, palm

up. An invitation, but not one I'm going to accept until he answers my questions. Childish, probably. But I never get that lucky, and I *live* there.

"Question one, someone was pulling out as I was pulling in, so I was lucky. Question two, I'm a country boy. I can fit this truck anywhere I need it to be." He pauses, looks over at me and winks. "And last question...it's a surprise. You'll just have to wait and find out."

He turns the radio on, and country music plays quietly in the background. Not loud enough to deter conversation, but enough to fill the silence. He pulls onto the highway and starts to drive us out of Dallas.

"You won't even give me a hint?" I plead.

"Nope, just sit back and enjoy the ride."

"Where are you from? I'm going on a date with you, and I don't even know where you live."

Chuckling, he glances at me. "Don't you have my address in your files at the shop? You know from when you made a copy of license?"

Why the hell didn't I think to look at his paperwork? "I didn't think to look. Are you hiding some deep dark secret?"

A shadow passes over his face, but it's gone before I can say anything, making me wonder if I imagined it. "Nope. I live thirty minutes south of here in a little town called Asheville."

I've never heard of it, but I don't leave the city much. Why would I when everything I need is literally ten minutes away from me, or can be delivered?

I lean back in the seat, listening to the soft crooning

coming from the speakers, and watch the lights of Dallas fade into the distance.

* * *

It doesn't take long to get to our destination, twenty maybe twenty-five minutes. But I squeal, when we pull up to a carnival. I'm so happy I decided not to wear my wedges because my feet would likely be aching at the end of the night. A ferris wheel and a multitude of rides light up the dark space where we're parking.

"I can't decide if you are brilliant or insane." I whisper yell. "I haven't been to a carnival since I was a kid."

And it's true, I haven't. I used to go with Mom and Dad all the time when I was a kid. But, I traded that in for days spent at the shop watching Corey work his magic. I don't notice that Jake has gotten out of the truck until I pull the handle and almost hit him with the door in my excitement.

"Are you surprised?" he asks.

"Yes. As far as first dates, this might be one of the best." I throw my arms around his neck and hug him. He stiffens, not expecting the movement, but quickly relaxes. Wrapping his arms around my waist and embracing me.

"Good," he whispers. "I wasn't sure if it was a good idea or not, but you can thank Marshall for convincing me to go with it."

"Maybe I'll tattoo him, no charge."

"No offense, but I don't think he'd like the

SpongeBob to match my Patrick," he laughs.

We walk hand in hand to the ticket booth. The lights becoming brighter the closer we get. I can see them bouncing in Jake's eyes when I sneak glances at him. I'm completely surprised that he had this in him. I know I don't really *know* him, but first impressions say a lot. I'm happy that he's not who I had him pegged as in my mind.

He's buying tickets, and my eyes wander around the carnival, trying to decide which ride I want to drag him on first.

Tickets in hand, I pull him toward the ferris wheel. It's always been my favorite. I remember sitting next to my dad and feeling like I was queen of the world when we would stop at the top. The people and booths so very small below us.

Luckily there isn't a line. I look to Jake for the tickets, but his face is pale. "Do you not like heights?"

"No," he pauses. "I'm good with heights." He turns to the ticket taker to give him the amount posted on the sign.

We climb into the chair, and while the person running the ride makes sure we are fastened in, I take Jake's hand. It's clammy, on the verge of being downright sweaty. "Are you sure you're okay? We don't have to ride this if you don't want to."

"I'm fine, Charleigh." He flashes me the same charming smile he gave me the night I tattooed him, but I see the fear in his eyes.

The chance to get off the ride is taken from us, and we start gliding backward. The higher we go, the stronger Jake's grip on my hand becomes. It's almost painful, but I don't want him to lose any sense of security he finds in me.

We stop at the top, and instead of enjoying the view like I used to as a child, I look over at Jake. "You obviously aren't okay with being up here."

He's trying his best to look anywhere but the ground.

"Focus on me," I lean in closer to him. "Why did you agree to the ride if you're terrified of heights?"

"Because you wanted to ride this death trap," he replies.

"You could have told me no. It wouldn't have broken my heart or anything."

"I know, but I want this to be an amazing date for you. So amazing that you'll agree to a second one."

This is one of those moments you dream about as a teenager. The ones you only see in movies and can't help but swoon over. I'm not sure what comes over me, but I scoot closer to him, place my hands on his cheeks, and kiss him.

I pull away long enough to mutter, "Anyone who will put their fears aside to impress a girl, definitely deserves a second date."

This time...he pulls me to him. His tongue sweeps across my lips, asking my permission, waiting for me to part my lips wider. And I do. Everything else fades away as his tongues glides around mine, setting all my senses on fire.

I'm not sure where this is going to go. But right now, I am so glad I text him, and I don't want this night to end.

jake

I OPEN MY EYES, slowly taking in my surroundings. There are frames with people I don't know, though I pick out Charleigh and Corey in a few of them. But those aren't what draw my attention. It's the artwork pinned randomly on the walls, unmistakably Charleigh's creations.

I can't believe I fell asleep here last night. She wasn't kidding when she said she didn't want the night to end. We stayed clear of the rest of the rides after my ferris wheel freak out. I told her I was fine, but I think she felt bad about dragging me on there when I was clearly uncomfortable.

She kept finding games to play, and try to beat, even though they are rigged. I even managed to win her one of those giant teddy bears, and I won't mention how much I spent to get it. It wasn't cheap, but it was worth it. Seeing Charleigh hug that damn bear made me beam with pride.

After stuffing ourselves we food, I dropped her off

with every intention of going home. She grabbed my hand when we got to her door, and she asked me to come in. The rest of the night was spent watching comedy shows on Netflix until we apparently fell asleep.

I look down and see a mass of hair. How in the hell can she still breathe with all that hair in her face? As gently as I can I brush her hair aside until she comes into view. She looks so peaceful in her sleep, and I'm not sure how I'm supposed to get off this couch without waking her up.

I'm surprised we both fit on it to be honest. Her entire body takes up most of the surface, and her feet are hanging over the edge. I'm halfway sitting on it, one foot on the floor, and a leg curled on the couch. She's lying on my leg. I try to lift most of her hair up so that it doesn't get caught between my leg and the couch, but as soon as I move my leg, she starts to stir.

I freeze. I don't know why. It's not like I plan on skipping out on her without saying goodbye, but I also didn't want to wake her. I figure she's got a long night ahead of her at the shop, and I want to make sure she's well rested. I'm trying to be a gentleman, something I've learned from past mistakes with Tonya. I need to be better...for myself, Charleigh, and Layla.

Charleigh sits up rapidly, almost hitting me in the face. She's pushing all the hair out of her face, yet again, and looks absolutely adorable. Her hair is sticking out in every direction, eyes wide, and hand wiping across her mouth. I'm assuming to make sure there's no drool present, but it wouldn't change the way I see her.

Blinking a couple of times, she says. "Morning. Did I wake you up?"

I must look dazed but seeing her to start my day is definitely a good thing. "Nope, I was trying to figure out how to get up without waking you." I stand up and nearly fall. The blood rushing back into the leg she was sleeping on, causing needles of pain up and down it.

Her smile turns into a small frown, eyebrows dropping lower. "You weren't even going to say bye?"

Shit. That was the wrong thing to say. I need to think before I speak. "I was going to, but you looked so peaceful. I didn't want to disturb you."

That mollifies her, at least a little bit. "Oh." She pushes a piece of hair behind her ear settling back into the couch. "Do you want to do something today?"

"I can't today. I have some things I have to do," I reply. If it were any other day I would love nothing more than to spend the day with her. But, today is not that day. I glance at my watch. I'm supposed to meet Tonya in a few hours so I can get more time with Layla. I'm going to put my daughter first, unlike my parents. I mean, they did put me first in a lot of ways, but not for the right reasons. I refuse to allow myself to end up like them.

I see Charleigh's shoulders sag. I really hope she doesn't think that I'm trying to ghost her because I'm not. I just don't want to drag her into what's going on in my life right after our first date. "I'll text or call you when I'm done. Maybe if you're not at work yet, we can hang out."

She nods and quietly says, "Okay."

I walk toward her, squatting down so that I can look

into her downcast eyes. "I'll call you." I place my hands on hers, until she looks directly at me. "Besides," I smirk. "You already agreed to a second date. You can't take that back."

Finally, I get a small giggle from her. "Actually, I can." She pauses, weaving her fingers through mine. "But I won't. I mean, what other guy would be okay with Netflix and chill without taking the "chill" as an invitation for something more."

Now it's my turn to laugh. "A make-out session would have been nice, just sayin'."

"It's not my fault you fell asleep."

Another chuckle, "You have a point there. But, I really need to go."

She rises as I stand up and throws her arms around me, nearly knocking me back. "Thanks for last night," she whispers in my ear. "I had an amazing time."

"You're welcome, Charleigh," I reply. "I had a great time, too. Even on that God forsaken ride."

I lean in to kiss her, but she rears back. "You can't kiss me right now. I haven't even brushed my teeth."

Chuckling, I say, "Well it's a good thing that I haven't either."

Before she has a chance to protest, I pull her to me. I kiss her long and slow, making sure she knows I'm still interested. Morning breath, and all.

I give her a kiss on the cheek. "I'll talk to you later."

I head to the door, scooping my keys from the coffee table on my way. "I look forward to it" are the last words I hear before closing the door behind me.

I expect there to be a ton of traffic while walking to

my truck, but it's oddly quiet. I'm used to this in my small town and didn't think it would be the same in a bigger city. It gives me time to think. Everything in my life seems to be lining up, but I'd be lying to myself if I said this playdate with Layla isn't making me nervous. Reaf will be there and I don't know how Layla is going to react with the both of us in the same space.

Will she choose him over me? I can already feel the sting of jealousy building in the pit of my stomach, and it hasn't even happened yet. How am I supposed to get over that and make this work?

There's only one way to find out. I just hope I can keep my emotions under control.

I pull into one of the few parking spaces available at the Asheville public park. I've never been more grateful that Marshall and I wear the same size clothes. I stopped by his house to freshen up on the way here to avoid my parents. I don't want to face another inquisition.

I see Tonya and Reaf spreading out a blanket on the lush green grass. I have no clue how they keep the grass alive with the high temperature here, but I'm kind of impressed. There's a stroller beside them that no doubt holds Layla.

I sit in my truck for a few moments, attempting to get my nerves under control. My leg is jittering in an unsteady rhythm as I watch them get everything set for me to arrive. I know I have no reason to be nervous. She did fine when I was at Tonya's house, but it was just us there. I reach for the handle, forcing myself to pull it open. I haven't seen them together since Spring Break. And I haven't interacted with the both of them since I acted like an ass in the fall.

I walk toward them, taking my time. Reaf notices me first, and simply nods in my direction. Tonya is getting Layla out of the stroller and placing her on the blanket with a myriad of toys. Why does she need so many toys? It's not like she's mobile, yet. But, I'm going to keep my mouth closed on that subject. I don't really have to right to voice my opinion when I'm just now getting to know my daughter.

"Hi, guys," I wave awkwardly. My smile feels bigger than normal, and maybe slightly maniacal. I straighten my lips some so I don't freak them out.

Tonya beams. "Hi, Jake. We were just getting things situated."

Her smile is just as weird as mine was. I wonder if she had doubts that I would show up today. I know I've had my moments, but I told her I'd be here. "How's little Miss Layla doing this morning?"

I lie down on my stomach on the opposite end of the blanket so that she can see me when she lifts her head. She's on her belly, tiny fingers reaching toward the toys Tonya laid out in front of her. Picking up the ring toy next to my hand, I scoot it closer to her until her fingers wrap around it. She immediately shoves the toy in her mouth, working her gums over it.

I rear back, not sure what to do. I look up at Tonya with wide eyes, and she's laughing at me. She thinks putting her hand over her mouth hides it, but it doesn't. "What do I do?"

"Nothing," she says through a chuckle, trying to get her laughter under control. "All of her toys are basically fair game for her to chew on. Well, not really chew since she doesn't have teeth, but it soothes her."

"Oh, okay," I reply. "As long as it's not harmful, then she can chew to her heart's content."

I'm happy just being in her space. Tonya and Reaf leave us so I can have a little bit of quality time with Layla. I make faces at her, and even speak in that annoying baby talk, doing everything I can to make her smile. Snapping pictures of her toothless grin, soaking in these moments. She may not remember them, but I will.

All of a sudden Layla starts whimpering, then full on crying. I glance around trying to spot Tonya. Her and Reaf are on the swings making googly eyes at each other. "Um, Tonya," I call out. "She's getting angry, and I don't want her to turn into the baby version of The Hulk."

Tonya starts walking toward us, Reaf right behind her, checking her watch. "She's probably hungry."

I watch in fascination as Tonya prepares Layla's bottle. She even has this little contraption that heats the milk up. She's definitely a pro at this whole parent thing in my eyes.

She's checking the temperature of the milk on her wrist. "Do you want to feed her?"

I'm not sure if I do. How do I do this? But I don't want to miss anything else with my little girl so I take the bottle while Tonya picks her up to hand her to me. I cradle her in my arms, putting the bottle to her lips, but she's not having it. I lift her a little higher, sniffing to see if she might be dirty, but she's not. Her diaper doesn't feel weighed down. I'm not sure what I'm doing wrong.

Reaf swoops in. "Do you want me to hold her while Tonya gets situated to feed her?"

I don't know what else to do, so I just nod, and lift my arms out for him to take her. Barely a few seconds have passed, and she's quieted down. A few whimpers escaping her lips.

Reaf passes Layla to Tonya so she can eat, and I'm quietly hurting. I know it's not his fault. I know I shouldn't get mad that Layla calms down when someone she's been around her entire three and a half months of living holds her, but it's hard. Seeing my baby girl find comfort in someone that's not me...it's like a punch to the gut.

I look at Reaf. I'm not really mad at him, just at the situation. The way his shoulders sag, and the way he's avoiding looking at me, tells me he feels horrible. That right there is why I'm grateful that out of all the guys out there, me included, she picked someone who's sensitive to how others feel.

I slowly stand up. Not really wanting to leave, but also not wanting them to see how much I'm bothered by what happened. "I'm going to head out."

"Are you sure?" Tonya's frowning. Not because she's upset I'm leaving, but because I think she knows how I'm feeling. Hell, she may even be proud of me for not letting my frustration get the best of me.

"Yeah, I've got a couple of things I need to do," I

shrug. I'm trying for nonchalant, but I know I'm not pulling it off.

I bend down to kiss Layla's head. Telling them bye, I turn for my truck. I've never been one to cry, but I'm fighting back the liquid pooling in my eyes. Wishing I would have gone about this differently from the beginning.

charleigh

THERE IS ABSOLUTELY nothing that can bring me down today. I have my first actual client coming into the shop in an hour. I'm practically bouncing off the walls I can barely contain my excitement. I need to bring it down a notch or she may spot me for the newbie that I am.

I grab the broom and begin sweeping the main room, glancing around to see what else needs to be straightened up. Anything to work off some of this nervous energy. At this point I don't even care what tattoo I'm doing, I'm just happy to finally be putting ink on someone.

The swish of the broom across the floor seems to be doing the trick, but my mind starts wandering to Jake. He texted me Saturday night like he said he would, but we didn't really go back and forth too much. He was tired, and we were swamped with people walking in. That hasn't happened in a while, but there is an arts festival going on, so we get an influx of customers when other shops have to turn them away.

We had so many we were having to do the same. My night was full of giving people forms to fill out, making copies of their licenses, and making sure Corey, Bianca, and Adrian had everything they needed. By the time I got home I was exhausted. I collapsed on my bed without even changing.

I was surprised to get an actual phone call from Jake yesterday. He doesn't strike me as the type to spend hours on the phone, but we did. He sounded a little sad, though. I didn't want to press him about it because we've only been on one date, but I can't help feeling like something major happened. I wanted to console him, but I didn't know how to do that without knowing the reason why.

Bianca's sudden appearance stops me in my tracks. I will not let her put me in a funk before my appointment.

"I hope you don't fuck up your tattoo today," she sneers.

I smirk. "Why don't you worry about your own clients. I noticed Marshall hasn't been in here in a while."

"What does that have to do with anything?" she questions.

"Honestly, nothing," I say. "But he seemed like the type that would be in here as much as possible to get new ink, and yet he hasn't shown up in a few days. Did you mess up something on the addition you did for him?"

She winces. "That's none of your business." She starts to walk away but turns back around. "Just don't screw up the tattoo. We don't want any more incidents with cartoon characters."

How in the hell does she know that? My only guess is Marshall told her. I shrug and resume sweeping. When I'm done, I put the broom away, and start setting up my station for my client, Sophia, to come in. I have no idea what she's going to get, but I can't wait to get started.

I'm putting the last typography print on the wall of my workroom when I hear the bell above the door jingle. The frame almost slips from my hands, but I manage to hang onto it. I finally find the hook it needs to sit and slide the picture on it. I dust my hands off like I did some sort of major construction instead of just sticking a hook and frame on the wall.

Adrian calls my name from the front room, and I take one final glance at my station before walking toward the counter. There's a timid girl standing on the other side. She has on those big framed glasses that most people associate with hipsters, long straight brown hair, and wide doe eyes. She looks terrified that she's here.

Adrian glances at me. "Charleigh, this is Sophia, your appointment." He points at her, and I can't tell if she wants to run screaming in the other direction or climb him like a tree. I see equal parts attraction and fear. And, can't help the grin that takes over my face.

"Hi, Sophia," I extend my hand out to her. "I'm Charleigh."

She takes my hand, giving it a gentle squeeze. "I'm Sophia. But you obviously know that already."

Looking over at Adrian, I don't miss the way he studies her. He's in his late twenties, and a good-looking guy. I wonder if he'll ask questions about her after our session. "Did you get Sophia to fill out the paperwork?"

"Yep, it's all right here," he hands me a clipboard. But he doesn't take his eyes off Sophia the entire time. "You're good too go."

"Thanks. Follow me back, Sophia." I don't wait to see if she's going to follow and walk to my room. Looking over the clipboard I note that she's twenty-four. She doesn't look it. Her skin is close to flawless, and she has a baby face. You know, the ones that will no doubt be carded for most of their adult lives. I try to merge my view of the mousy girl standing before me, and the one that wants to permanently ink her skin.

I catch myself in the mirror. Anybody looking at me would assume I'm a straight-laced girl, with zero tattoos, and dreams of a normal nine to five job. They would be wrong. Who am I to try to see who this girl is without getting to know her? The small reality check is exactly what I need to put my mind in the right place.

Sophia walks into the workroom and stops dead in her tracks. She's looking at all the walls and bright colors. I can't help but laugh. "Did you expect something different?"

She nods. "I figured it's be a bit more broody and tortured artist."

"Eh," I shrug. "Broody isn't really my thing." Like I said to myself before...it's all about perception.

I motion her toward the chair, "So, what are you wanting to do today?"

Sophia sits, wringing her hands. "There's two that I want, but I'm not sure how I want them done." Her knee is bouncing with nerves. "I was hoping you could help me with that."

She's really nervous. It's written in her posture, and the fact that she can't sit still. There's only one reason for her reaction. "Sophia, have you ever gotten a tattoo before?"

"No," she shakes her head. "Is it that obvious?"

"A little," I laugh. "But it's all good. We've all been there before, I just had the luxury of growing up in this place so I knew what to expect."

"Will it hurt?"

"That depends." I sigh, "For some it can, but it's more annoying than anything else." Pausing, I study her. I don't want to tattoo her if she's going to freak out, but I understand where she's coming from. "Do you still want to do this?"

She doesn't answer right away, but I see the moment she decides she wants it in her eyes. There's a resolve there, and I'm sure she's one of those people that has put a lot of thought into getting a tattoo.

"Let's do this," Sophia exclaims.

"That's what I like to hear." I can't help the huge grin that takes over my face.

She tells me what she wants the wording to say and start adding my own flair to my sketch pad. I get her enthusiastic approval of my design and begin transferring to the carbon paper.

"What made you decided on these specific tattoos?"

"Well," she pauses. "The 'Always' is from Harry Potter, of course. I've loved that series since I was a child, and it helped me through some pretty crappy situations in school. The other is my little reminder to myself after reading a book called *Revelry*."

I nod, listening to everything she has to say. "I've never heard of it. I'm guessing you had a connection to it?"

"You could say that." She takes a sip of water from her bottle before continuing, "I had just come out of a pretty rough relationship. And, I felt, I don't know like I wasn't worth anything. I lost myself. But this book, it spoke to me. It made me realize that I I'm so much more."

"You might be my new favorite client." I don't tell her that she's technically my first one. I refuse to count Jake's tattoo as my first, even though I still find it hysterical weeks later. "Most people come in here and get tattoos that hold no meaning to them. They just felt like doing it. But you...you have put so much thought into this. I can't wait to see what you think."

I've just transferred the first design onto Sophia's wrist when my phone dings with a message.

Jake: What are you doing right now?

> *Charleigh: About to tattoo someone. Talk later?*

Jake: No SpongeBob!

Jake: Call me when you're done?

> *Charleigh: She actually knows what she wants. No weird cartoon tats for her. I'll call you.*

· · ·

I'm so happy that he can laugh about the Patrick tattoo. Not many people would be able to. I just knew he was going to call Corey raising hell. Instead he slowly worked his way into asking me for a date.

"You ready?" I ask Sophia. "You can still sit in that chair, but I'm going to need you to lean your arm across the table."

"Okay," she swallows so hard I can see her throat move.

"You're going to do great." I squeeze her hand to reassure her. "Just let me know if you need a break, and I'll stop."

"Sounds good." A small smile appears on her face. I just know this girl is going to love tattoos as much as I do.

I pull a pair of gloves out of the box and shove my hands into them. I hate the way they feel, but it's a requirement. I connect the power to the gun then dip it into the small pot of ink and press the footswitch so that Sophia can get used the sound.

The moment I start tracing the lines of the design, Sophia jerks. It's startling when you get your first one. But soon she's relaxed and talking to keep her nerves at bay. And me? I'm in my element.

jake

IT'S BEEN over a week since I've seen Charleigh. I've wanted to go to the shop and see her, but I know she's busy. Since her uncle has given her more clients, she's been incredibly busy. I'm ready to see her today, though. Evenings are hard since they are open late.

My phone sitting on the dresser dings, and I rush over hoping it's Charleigh, but also scared she might be cancelling on our second date. There was no need to hurry over, it's just Randall.

Randall: Lake in 30 minutes.

Jake: I can't. I have plans.

Randall: With that tattoo chick?

Jake: Does it matter?

Randall: Nope. But ditching us for a girl is pretty fucking stupid.

• • •

I haven't been hanging out with the guys lately, but it's not all because of Charleigh. They just assumed that, and I haven't corrected them. My time has been spent looking for a job. Preparing for the shit show that's going to take place when my parent's figure out I'm going to be in Layla's life, this isn't how I envisioned my summer. But I'll do whatever needs to be done to be a part of her world. My phone vibrates in my hand.

Randall: You know your parents are going to flip their shit when they meet her right?

Jake: Yep. Ask me if I care...

Randall: Whatever, dude. Don't forget about us while you're making googly eyes at her

Jake: I'll catch up with y'all tonight.

He doesn't reply. He's either pissed, doesn't care, or talking shit about me to the rest of the guys. I don't really care. The only one who understands is Marshall. The other two are too busy chasing their next conquest and getting sloppy drunk.

Glancing at the clock, I realize it's almost eleven and I need to get out of here if I'm going to make it for lunch with Charleigh. I grab my keys and run down the stairs. At least I don't have to deal with the parents today. Since it's the middle of the day on a Wednesday, they are at work, and I couldn't be more grateful.

I've been avoiding them at all costs. Not wanting them to drag me into another fight about Tonya. I don't understand why they are so worried about it. It's not like I'm going to look to them to support my kid. Hell, I wouldn't even go to them for parenting advice. All they do is tell you what's expected and what isn't tolerated.

Looking back on my relationship with Tonya, I realize that my upbringing had a lot to do with why we failed as a couple. I acted like the spoiled brat that I am. Any time I've gotten into any kind of trouble my parents waved their cash around until the issue was dropped. God, I'm such a douchebag. It's taken me way too long to realize it. But today is another day to put my feet in the right direction.

Charleigh doesn't even come to the door when I knock. I'm standing there, shuffling my feet, wondering if she forgot about our lunch date. There's no way she could have forgotten. I double checked with her last night that we were on for today, and she doesn't seem like the type of person to stand someone up.

"Come in," Charleigh calls from somewhere in her apartment. "The doors unlocked."

Pushing the door open, I holler back, "I'm pretty sure that's not a smart thing to call out."

She walks out of her bedroom in a fluffy robe and a towel wrapped around her head. Her long legs draw my attention, and I can't help staring. Looking her over from her blue painted toes, all the way to the top of the towel, I feel incredibly lucky that she decided to give me a chance.

"Yo," she snaps her fingers. "My eyes are up here."

"Um, sorry."

"I barely unlocked it five minutes ago if you were wondering." She shakes her hair loose of the towel and her wavy hair surrounds her face. "Besides, I wasn't expecting anyone else."

I laugh, "I don't think a serial killer would care if you were expecting them or not."

"True," she pauses. "But I don't think they would knock at all."

Touche. "You aren't dressed."

"I know. I'm sorry."

"It's okay, I just didn't want you to be late for work."

"I got in late last night and slept through my alarm this morning. Let me go get dressed really quick."

She throws the towel in an overflowing basket right outside her door. She starts untying her robe as she passes through the door but is around the corner before I assume she takes it off to put on whatever she's wearing. A small, okay big, part of me is disappointed her robe didn't slip to the floor sooner, but I don't want to be *that* guy. The one that is all about the physical and none of the emotional aspects of a relationship. I'm trying to be different than before, but right now she's making that incredibly hard.

I don't know what to do while I wait. Sitting here twiddling my thumbs doesn't sound like a good idea. My mind will just wonder how Charleigh looks under that robe. A little tour around her apartment seems like a good way to use my time. It will give me a peek into who she is outside of the tattoo shop.

The kitchen is full of mismatched appliances, dishes and knick-knacks. My mother would have a heart attack because of that alone. Some of the dishes are older, but she has a few square modern plates sitting in the cabinet. All of the counters, and cabinets, are painted white, but they look distressed on purpose. It's a definitely a shock from the sleek, lifeless look of my kitchen.

Opening the only cabinet that doesn't have a glass door, I peek inside. There is a box of Fruit Loops with marshmallows. Blegh, that doesn't even sound like a good combination. What sort of weirdo am I dating?

It feels good saying that. It's been a long time since I've even considered dating anyone. Even back before I confronted Tonya about us getting back together. I didn't want to be with anyone. I didn't even really want to be with Tonya if I'm being honest with myself. I was just doing what I thought was the right thing to do. What my parents told me I needed to do.

Charleigh comes back into the living room while I'm getting a closer look at the art she has pinned around the mirror. She has a thing for feathers if the ones all over the pages are any indication. They draw you in, though. They are vivid, and you can see each individual piece of the feather.

"These are really good," I say loud enough so she can hear me.

I jump when she places a hand on my shoulder. "Thanks."

"You are like a fucking ninja," I laugh. My words die on my lips the moment I turn around.

Charleigh is wearing a sundress with skulls all over.

The perfect outfit for the date I have planned for us. It also shows off the half sleeve tattoos she has on both arms. The left side is a colorful nod to *Alice in Wonderland*, hats, tea cups, and clocks woven together beautifully. Her right arm has a mixture of flowers, skulls, and feathers in black with shading to tie it all together.

"I love your tattoos," I whisper.

Her cheeks turn a bright red. A small smile appearing on her face. "I designed them and Corey did the tattoos."

She lifts her hands to cover her face, but I grab them and pull her into me. Lifting her chin up, I make sure I have her full attention. "Don't be embarrassed. They are a part of you." I grin, "And, if your reaction to my tattoo is any indication, you put a lot of thought and work into them."

She leans forward until her head is on my chest. "Thank you." Wrapping her arms around my waist she continues, "I'm not embarrassed, but I never know how people who aren't fans of tattooing are going to react."

"You don't have to worry about that with me," I murmur into the hair piled atop her head. "I like you just the way you are."

"Good." She smacks my butt and jumps back. "Now, let's get this date started." Grabbing her bag, she leads the way to the door. "And, please tell me food is involved. I'm starving."

"Alright, alright. Let's go feed you." I roll my eyes. "So, demanding."

* * *

Going to the park to see Layla gave me an idea for this date with Charleigh. Yep, we are going on a picnic. It's nothing fancy. I picked up a few things to make sandwiches on my way to pick her up. I'm not trying to wow her this time. I want to get to *know* her.

We arrive at White Rock Lake, and I pull the blanket I brought from the back seat. Jumping out of the truck, I rush around to the passenger side to open the door for Charleigh.

"We aren't doing any outdoorsy activity, are we?" She asks while stepping down.

"Nope. We're going to have lunch right over there under that tree."

I picked this place because it's kind of close to her apartment, and because it has *trees*. Shade is a must today. It's barely after lunch and already the heat has me melting. Maybe coming to the park during summer wasn't my best plan. But I didn't want to be in a restaurant where we would have to compete with the everyday chatter just to hear each other.

Pulling the ice chest out of the bed of my truck I almost drop everything else in my hands. Charleigh rushes over, trying to take the ice chest from me. "I've got it," I say.

She leans back, crosses her arms over her chest, and arches one eyebrow. How in the hell do people do that? I'm going to have to practice that move. "Obviously," she deadpans, pointing at the blanket dragging at my feet.

I drop the ice chest to the ground. "Fine, you can carry the blanket and my keys."

"I thought you didn't need any help," she teases.

"Smart ass," I murmur under my breath.

"I heard that," she calls back. "Better to be a smart ass than a dumbass."

Women...how is it they can hear everything you mutter? As soon as we get under the branches of the tree, I let the ice chest plop to the ground. I think one bag of ice would have been enough. It definitely would have this thing a hell of a lot lighter.

Charleigh lifts the lid, moving things around, looking to see what all I've packed.

"I'm perfectly capable of putting together a picnic, you know."

"I can see that," she smirks. She begins putting together a couple of sandwiches for us, not giving me a chance to intervene. She also doesn't ask what I like on mine. When she squirts a ginormous amount of mustard onto my bread, I cringe. I'm a mayo type of guy. But when she hands me sandwich, I don't make a big deal about it. I take a huge bite, doing my best to swallow without making a face.

But she sees right through it. "You're one of those weirdos that doesn't like mustard, aren't you?"

"Nah, I love it."

"Dude, you look like your about to puke." She's laughing at me.

"I'm going to finish this sandwich because you made it. Mustard be damned." My smile is wide, and I know my cheeks are puffed out because of course I'm mid chew when I make the proclamation.

"You do that."

I finish the sandwich in four big bites, doing my best

to eat it as fast as I can while also trying not to offend her. I take a swig of water to wash the taste out of my mouth.

"Sooo," I draw out. "What made you get into tattooing?"

She smirks, "Is this an interview or something?"

"Just trying to get to know you a little better." I shrug. "Isn't that what you do when you're dating someone? Ask questions?"

She rolls her eyes and takes a drink of water. "I guess. But it's really not all that interesting." Putting the cap back on her water bottle she continues, "I spent a lot of time watching my uncle work. I was fascinated by the art he created, and he always encouraged me to do what makes me happy. And being a tattooist at Life in Ink is my happy spot."

"You can tell you've grown up with that kind of influence. It shows in the pride you take in your work. What do your parents think?"

She shrugs her shoulders and sighs. "They're supportive for the most part."

"I sense a but coming."

"But...they think I should go back to school and at least some sort of degree." She takes another drink of water. "I can see their point, and I'm thinking about it. A degree in marketing would really help get the shop's name out there, but I don't want to try to juggle it all either. What about you?"

"I've got a football scholarship and majoring in law."

"I have a feeling that's not what you want to do."

"Honestly, I don't know what I want to do." I want to

tell her about Layla but I don't know how. And, I'm pretty sure it's too early to even discuss children. What if I tell her and she runs for the hills? I don't want whatever this is to end before it even begins.

"What about your parents? Are they the ones pushing you toward a law degree?" She questions.

"My parents are overbearing assholes. They only care about themselves and appearances."

She puts her hands under chin. "Well, I hope I never have the pleasure of meeting them."

"I'll try my best to save you from their presence." I really hope they never meet. Not because I'm ashamed of Charleigh, but because I don't want her to become a target of their criticism.

The temperature is slowly rising, and even though the tree offers us some relief, I don't want to subject her to the heat any longer.

"You ready to get out of here. I don't want you to melt."

"Sure, I need to get ready for work anyway."

We gather everything up and throw our trash away. I rush to get the air conditioner blowing when we get in the truck. It might be hot as hell outside, but seeing Charleigh enjoy my simple picnic means a lot to me.

I want to linger when we get to her building, but I don't. Not wanting to get too attached too quickly, I give her a kiss and tell her bye. Before I make it to the truck, I'm texting Randall, seeing which lake they are at. A night with the guys is way overdue.

charleigh

THE PAST FEW weeks Jake and I have either seen each other, or talked, every single day. He's the one I go to when I have news to share. He's also the one who gets to hear about Bianca the most. Since I've started doing more tattoos, she's been meaner and nastier. Every single day she has something to say.

It's to the point I'm considering asking Corey to switch our schedules. Or, at the very least make the hours I work with her shorter. It might mean less money for me, but it will keep the comments I have to endure to a minimum.

Don't get me wrong. I'm no delicate flower. I participate in our little verbal song and dance just to see what craziness comes out of her mouth. It just gets old. She doesn't treat anyone else the way she treats me. I just wish I knew what is so horrible about me that she feels the need to harp on me about every little thing.

The only saving grace has been Sophia. She came back three times after that initial tattoo for more ink. I knew in my gut that she'd be one of those that absolutely loves them. The last time she was in my chair, Corey came in complaining about nobody being up front to take appointments. She was looking for a new job, and he hired her on the spot. Well, after I finished the tattoo I was working on.

"Hey, girlfriend," I walk into the lobby. "I'm going to grab lunch do you want anything?" Sophia is staring at the door to Adrian's workroom. I'm not a hundred percent sure she even knows I'm in the room with her.

Walking over to the counter I snap my fingers in front of her face. "Earth to Sophia, is anyone in there?"

She jumps, clearly surprised by my appearance. "Oh, uh sorry, did you say something?"

"Girl, you've got it bad."

Her cheeks flush. "I don't know what you're talking about." She starts shuffling papers on the counter.

"Sure, you don't," I say, but I don't say anything else. She doesn't need me telling her what her feelings are, even though I can see them from a mile away.

I know what adoration looks like. I see it every time Marshall comes into the shop for more work with Bianca. The huge smile that takes over his face, and the eagerness that shines in his eyes. It's not much different than the look Sophia has any time Adrian talks to her or looks her way.

"Did you need something?" Sophia asks.

"Do you want me to get you something to eat while I'm out?"

"No, I'm good."

"Okay, I'll be back in just a bit." Walking outside, I

immediately want to turn right back around and order in. The heat is stifling and walking to the burger place down the street seems like a horrible idea right now. But, I *need* to get away from Bianca for a bit. She's in full on bitch mode today.

That leads me back to Marshall. I've noticed that she's almost pleasant when he's been in the shop. I've suspected they have something going on, but it's a pattern I've noticed. I wonder what's going to happen when Marshall goes back to school in the fall. Will they try the whole long-distance thing? Or, will he drop her like a sack of potatoes and leave us to deal with her wrath?

What will happen when Jake goes back to school? The thought has never even crossed my mind. I guess I knew deep down that he wouldn't be here after the summer, but damn that was before I had any actual feeling for him. Before I got to know him. And, still I know there's something he's not telling me. I wonder if I'll find out before he leaves. If I'll be able to watch him go, and not let it affect me. What will happen to us?

I stop dead in my tracks, right before reaching the door of the restaurant. When did I start thinking about a future with him? This is exactly why I don't get involved with people. Will he expect me to move if we want to stay together? I finally got started on my career, I can't let a guy determine how the rest of my life is going to go.

My back pocket starts vibrating, scaring the living daylight of out of me. Scooting to the side, so I don't block the path, I slide my phone from my pocket and answer it. Not even looking to see who is calling.

"Hello."

"Hi, Sweetie," Mom says sweetly from the other side of the phone.

Uh oh, she never starts with that. She usually asks how my day is or what I'm doing.

"Hi, Mom."

"Have you thought any more about going back to school? I have a few brochures I can give you. I can –"

I cut her off before she even has a chance to finish whatever she was going to say. I have thought about it, mostly to help the shop grow. Some of the social media I've talked Corey into implementing is working, which is why we're so busy. But...I'm not telling her that.

"Is that really the only reason you called?" I ask.

She sighs, knowing she's already lost me on this subject. "Yes. I just think you need to consider your future if tattooing doesn't work out."

"Mom," I rub the temples of my head trying to ease the headache that is forming. "I've been doing a lot of tattoos. We're so packed that we had to hire someone just to take appointments."

"Well, that's good."

"And," I relent. "I am thinking about at least taking online courses in marketing. It'll help get more visibility on the shop, *and* should I ever need to get another job, I will be able to."

"I'm so happy you're considering it." I can hear the smile in her voice. She may not like my profession, but at least I can lessen her worries over me by doing this one thing.

"I'm grabbing lunch right now, I'll call you soon." I

hang up because I know if I let her say anything else, we'll be on the phone for another hour.

Finally, I open the door and walk to the counter. My little freak out and Mom calling ate away some of my time.

"What can I get you?" The lady behind the counter asks. She must be new because I've never seen her before.

"Hi," I reply. "I need a burger with everything but onions on it and two orders of fries, please."

"Absolutely."

I hand over my debit card before she has a chance to give me my total. I wait by the order pick up area looking around the restaurant. I've always loved this place. Aunt Nikki, Corey's wife, would always bring burgers to the shop when we were too wrapped up in designing.

Before I get too wrapped up in nostalgia, Ginger sets my bag of food on the bar. "Here you go Charleigh. You tell your uncle not to work too hard. Him and Nikki haven't been here in a while."

I laugh. It's true, but that's only because we've been swamped. "I will." I loop the handle over my wrist, "Bye, Ginger."

She waves at me, and as I reach for the handle my phone starts ringing again. I fumble to answer it, almost dropping my food. "I don't have time right now, Mom."

"Would you like me to call you back later?" a deep voice comes through the speaker. It's Jake.

"Oh, sorry. I thought it was my mom bugging me about college again," I say sheepishly. He must have felt me thinking about him. He'll usually send a text asking if I can talk. Him just calling is out of the ordinary.

"It's okay," he replies. "But, really, I can call you back when you have time."

He sounds different., almost sad. I can't tell him to call back when he's down. "It's okay. Is everything okay?"

"Oh, yeah," he says. He's lying, but I'm not going to call him out for it. "Just some shit with my parents I'm dealing with."

My phone is filled with silence. I can hear him breathe, but that's about it. We've never had a problem with awkward silences. It's weird, and I'm not sure how to react to that.

"Actually," he begins, "I was calling to see if you wanted to come hang-out with me and my friends tonight."

"I can't tonight. I'm working." I pause, feeling bad that I can't go out with him tonight. I've only met his friends once, aside from Marshall, whom I see almost more than I see Jake. "But, I'm off tomorrow night if that works."

"Yeah, that's fine. We'll do the bonfire tomorrow night." He takes a deep breathe, blowing it out right into the receiver. "I just...I just needed to see you. But I can wait." Defeat tinges his voice.

"You know you can talk to me about whatever is bothering you, right?"

"Yeah," he's silent once again. "I'm gonna let you go so I can help the guys gather the stuff for tomorrow night. Text me when you get home?"

"Yeah, I'll text you."

"I'll see you tomorrow."

We hang up, and I stare at my phone. That has to be the weirdest conversation we've ever had. Is he freaking out about what's going to happen at the end of the summer?

We seriously need to talk. I walk back into Life in Ink and set my food on the counter. I'm not sure what is going to happen tomorrow night, but I hope I get along with his friends, and he cheers up before then.

jake

I CAN'T BELIEVE they're getting married. It's the only thought running through my head as I throw broken tree limbs into the back of my truck. The limbs hitting the side of the truck, most likely scratching it up, isn't enough to distract me.

It's not even about them getting married, not *entirely*. I can't wrap my head around them getting engaged after being together barely over six months. Tonya and I were together off and on throughout most of high school and marriage never even crossed my mind. It's probably a good indicator that things between us probably never would have worked out. She wasn't my forever person.

Charleigh pops into my head. I wanted to see her so badly tonight. Just to focus on something good in my life. Focus on someone who makes me feel better and want to be a better person. But how can I when there's a twinge of jealousy burning in my gut?

I know he's been there for Layla since she was born. But it didn't bother me as much because he still went home to his own house. He wasn't always with her. Once they're married…they'll be living together as a family unit. I'll be relegated to the part-time dad. My opinions and concerns regarding Layla won't hold as much sway.

And why should I get a say? I haven't put in anywhere near as much time into parenting her as they have. I haven't had to deal with sleepless nights or worry if her fever was too high. If I'm being honest, I would probably freak the hell out.

The day she was born, I knew I wanted to be more to her than my parents were to me. I don't even know if they planned on having me. I've always felt like more of a nuisance than their child. I never want Layla to feel that way when it comes to me. I want, no *need*, to be around as much as Tonya will allow me to be.

How am I going to do that from a university on the other side of the state? I don't have any other choice than to transfer to a school closer. And I'll do it because she is worth it. She's worth the world, and more.

"Yo, Jake," Randall cuts into my thoughts. "You're doing that weird staring thing again. Are you thinking about Charleigh?" He sing songs.

I shake my head, like it's going to rid me of all my problems. "Not right this second, no."

"You must be thinking about *her*," he argues.

"Jesus, Randall." I throw the limb in my hand to the ground. "I wish you'd stop talking about Tonya like she's Voldemort, or some evil overlord. She has a fucking name and happens to be the mother of my child. If you can't accept that, you can get your ass out of here."

"Yeah, and she chose another fucking guy to raise

your kid with. You aren't the one playing house with her, he is. I'm just sayin', it's messed up."

I rush toward him, fist raised, when Marshall steps between us and pushes me back.

Marshall's hand is pressed against my chest. "Calm down, Jake." He speaks low enough that only I can hear him.

"No," I push forward. "He has to stop this bullshit. Why does he think he can do people that way?"

Randall's laughter breaks through the air. "Oh, that's rich. You used to be just like me. Remember? That's the whole reason Tonya dumped your ass to begin with. So why don't you be a little more hypocritical?"

I. See. Red. It's taking all the strength Marshall has to keep me right where I am. "Dylan," he yells. "Want to get Randall out of here?"

"On it," Dylan calls back.

Soon I hear tires peeling out, then dust and gravel fly up, as Dylan does what Marshall asked.

"Dude, what the hell was that?" Marshall demands.

"I'm just tired of him always badmouthing Tonya." I lean against the truck, sliding down until my ass hits the ground. "She's never done anything to him."

"It's not himself he's worried about. He's looking out for you in his own weird way."

Leaning my head back, I grunt. "More like asshole way." I study Marshall. There's something he's not telling me, and I have a feeling I'm not going to like it. "Whatever it is your keeping from me, go ahead and spit it out."

"It's going to get out at some point," he mutters. "I think he may be projecting his emotions a little bit."

"Meaning...."

He sighs. "Meaning he had a thing for Tonya, and she chose you. He never even stood a chance, and it still gets to him."

"Are you serious?"

"Yep," he shrugs. "He doesn't want you to feel the way he did when Tonya wanted to be with you."

"That's so stupid. It's not even about her and Reaf."

"That's good since you're seeing Charleigh. But what is it about?"

I roll my eyes. It all seems so absurd now. "It's about my role in Layla's life. I'm not sure where I'll fit in when they get married."

"You realize that it's no different than now, right? You'll still be able to form and build a relationship with her." He joins me on the ground, leaning against the truck. "Tonya isn't going to keep Layla from you, neither of them of will. She's been a lot nicer than most people in this situation."

"I know. It's just weird, ya know. They haven't even been together a year."

Marshall laughs, "It may be weird, but you can't put a timeline on love. When you know, you know." He pauses. "Have you told Charleigh about Layla, yet?"

"Nope."

"Why not?"

"I don't want to give her a reason to run for the hills. I don't even know where we'll stand at the end of the summer. I'm supposed to go back to school, and I know she won't go with me." Marshall is giving me the condescending look he used to give me when I was a jerk to Tonya. I rush on, "Not that I'd ever ask her to give up everything she's worked so hard for."

"What do you mean 'supposed' to go back to school. Are you not going?"

"I'll probably transfer somewhere here. I need to be here if I'm going to be a part of Layla's life."

"Look at you being all grown up."

"Speaking of being grown up..." I begin. "What's going on with you and Bianca?"

"It's complicated."

I chuckle, "Isn't it always? She gives Charleigh a lot of shit when they're at work. I don't think she's a fan so I hope you aren't planning on inviting her to the bonfire."

"She has to work. She acts like she's a badass, but she's actually really nice. She dealt with a lot of crap to make a name for herself."

"If you say so, man."

Marshall stands and holds his hand out to me. "Let's get the last of the branches loaded up so we can set up the bonfire."

Thirty minutes later and we're pulling into the field. Dylan's car is next to the massive pit we've built for the bonfire. I don't see him or Randall, but I know they're around here somewhere.

I pull up next to Dylan and put my truck in park just as they emerge from the woods. Randall is holding his hand. He most likely had to blow off some steam and hit a damn tree. He may be a pain in the ass but I know he'd rather hurt himself than anyone else, even when he isn't in the wrong. He's the total opposite of his dad in every way. And I have nothing but respect for him because of that.

I step out of the truck and Dylan stands in front of Randall, worried I'm going to attack him. "Hey man, can we talk?"

Dylan looks at Marshall but he doesn't move until he gets some sort of signal that I'm not going to do anything rash.

Randall joins me at the front of the truck while Marshall and Dylan start unloading the brush.

"I'm sorry," I say holding my hand out, hoping he grabs it.

He looks down at my hand before grabbing it and giving it a quick shake before putting his hands in his pockets. "It's okay. I didn't mean any harm."

"I get it."

"Get what?" he asks.

"Marshall told me how you felt about Tonya." His face falls. "I'm not mad about it. And, I'm not in that same position. I know there's no future with Tonya, and I don't want to be with her anymore."

"Then why the hell did you blow up back there?"

Marshall and Dylan are very slowly pulling the brush out of the bed of the truck. Lingering so they can overhear what we're saying. I swear they are like a bunch of gossips just itching to know what's going on.

I motion them away and turn back to Randall. "A

bunch of irrational fears about Layla, and where that leaves me. But, I'm good now."

"Dude, anyone who's seen you with Layla knows you love her. And Tonya won't be a bitch about letting you see her, married or not."

"Thanks. We good?"

"Yeah," he pats me on the back. "We're good."

We finish unloading the limbs, setting them up for optimal burning tomorrow night. It's a good thing we got that rain earlier in the week or we wouldn't even be able to have this bonfire.

It's well after dark when everything is done. We're sitting around reminiscing about the good old days when we didn't have any worries, before I became a father, when my phone dings.

Charleigh: I made it home.

Jake: Good deal. Get some rest, I can't wait to see you tomorrow.

Charleigh: You seem like you're in a better mood.

Jake: My friends put me in my place.

Charleigh: Want to enlighten me?

Jake: Soon. You should sleep. I know you've been on your feet most of the day.

Charleigh: Okay...Goodnight

Jake: Goodnight, Beautiful

I'm not sure what time I make it home, but it feels good having that weight lifted off my shoulder. To know that my friends have my back, and that they believe every-thing will be okay.

Well as okay as it can be right now. In this moment... it's enough.

charleigh

THE PILES of clothes on my bed and floor are mocking me. I have no clue what one even wears to a bonfire, I've never been to one. There isn't really an opportunity to have them in the city.

I pick up a pair of skinny jeans in one hand and a pair of shorts in the other, determining the suitability of each garment. It's hot, even at night, the heat presses in on all sides. But what if there's tall grass? Jeans would be a better option to ward of the creepy crawlies. This decision should not be that hard.

There's a knock on the door, and I know it's Jake. Instead of hollering for him to come in, I walk to the door, still wrapped up in my towel, and open it.

He's leaning against the door jamb, smirking. "Why am I not surprised that you aren't ready?" His gaze moves up and down my body slowly. "And, you're only wearing a towel this time."

"Shut up," I lift my arm to throw my shorts at him. But he grabs it and pulls me to him. Wrapping me up in his arms. He lowers his head, and presses soft kisses to my neck, taking his time as he moves toward my lips.

As soon as his mouth touches mine, he devours me. He pushes one hand into my hair, fingers tangling in the still damp strands. His other arm is wrapped around my waist pulling me as close to him as possible. He is stranded in a desert, and I'm the fountain of water he needs to survive.

His tongue sweeps across mine. There's nothing else for me to do but drop the clothes in my hands, wrap my arms around his neck, and cling to him as he deepens the kiss.

He walks me backward until we're both in the apartment, pushing the door closed with his foot. When I think he's about to break what might be the best kiss I've ever received, he spins me until my back is flush with the door. Every inch of our bodies touching.

The desperation in the kiss slowly ebbs. He gives me one last peck, before leaning his forehead against mine. Our breaths mingling. "I've missed you."

I smile up at him, "I missed you, too." And if I get *that* greeting every time we see each other, I'm not going to complain. He damn near swept me off my feet.

I watch him study me, trying not to squirm from the ache building between my legs. This isn't the first time we've been in this situation. We've had some pretty heavy make-out sessions when we hang out here to watch movies. I've tried pressing him to go further, but he's remained a gentleman. Not wanting to push me too far. It's not pushing if I'm willing.

I push off the wall, and he steps back. Grabbing his

hand, I lead him past the sofa, and straight to my bedroom. The one place in my apartment he hasn't been.

I release his hand, waiting to see what he's going to do. He runs a finger through his hair and looks around the room like he's lost. Confusion written all over his face.

When he doesn't make a move, I walk to the nightstand and pull a condom out of the box I bought when I started catching feelings for him. He sees the foil packet in my hand, bites his lip and groans.

I take a few steps toward him, loosen the knot on my towel, and let it drop to the floor. His eyes widen, practically bugging out of his head. I know I'm not the only one that wants this, I can see the bulge in his jeans.

My freak out from yesterday still needs to be addressed, but right now...right now I want *him*.

I step closer to him, and all at once our hands are a flurry of action. I'm tugging his shirt over his head, and his hands are trying to touch every part of me they can. As soon as his clothes are littering the floor, he puts the condom on, and walks me to my bed. He pushes the clothes piled on top of it to the floor before guiding me back.

He leans over me, desire pouring off him in waves, and asks, "Are you sure?"

Cupping his face between my hands, I nod and whisper, "Yes."

In his eyes I see lust, but I also see adoration. And, I know I'm in trouble because I'm already falling for him, secrets and all. This may end up being a huge mistake, but right now I need to feel him.

That whispered confirmation is all he needs to show me exactly how much he missed me.

* * *

We pull onto a tiny gravel road in the middle of nowhere. Images of slasher movies pop into my head, and I realize this is how most of those movies begin. I subtly reach toward the door making sure it's locked. I study our surroundings as best I can in the pitch-black night just in a case a chainsaw wielding psychopath comes out of the darkness. I know that's highly unlikely but I need to know which direction to run in case it happens.

I reach over and grab Jake's hand, slipping my fingers through his. The memory of those hands caressing every part of my body only a couple of hours ago replaying through my mind. Gentle but firm, knowing exactly how I needed to be touched.

He glances at me, smiling. "We're almost there. Are you nervous?"

I snort. "Not at all. That mouthy friend of yours I sometimes hear in the background of our phones calls better watch out. He may end up junk punched by the end of the night."

He laughs so hard his body is shaking. "That would be Randall. I promise he's not that bad."

"If you say so," I mumble. Any time I've talked to Jake when he's with his friends, that guy is always loud and annoying. I don't know how Jake can stand to be friends with him sometimes.

Another chuckle comes from the driver's side. A

small grin crosses my face. It feels good to hear him laugh and see that small spark of humor light up his eyes. Especially after how sullen and lost he sounded yesterday.

Looking out the front window I see flicks of orange and yellow, rising up to meet the sky. As we get closer to the bonfire I hear country music filling the otherwise quiet air. I roll the window down to listen. It's not the new music they blast on the radio claiming to be country. No, this country has meaning. You can feel their emotions and thoughts through the lyrics, from a generation that's not our own. A generation that no doubt faced the problems we do but felt them on a level of maturity that we aren't capable of yet.

Jake pulls through a gate that I didn't even see. He must come out here a lot to know exactly where it is. There's a small group of people gathered around a large fire, hands grasping cans and bottles. They seem completely at ease, like this is a regular occurrence for them.

We park the truck and Jake comes around the front to open the door for me. It's something you don't see very often anymore. One thing I doubt I'll ever get used to is getting out of his truck. I still don't understand why he wanted it so high off the ground. He says it's so he can go mudding, whatever the hell that is, and it keeps him from getting stuck. Jake grabs my hand so that I can jump down without losing my footing.

Walking up to his group of friends, I grip his hand a little tighter. I may have lied a little bit about being nervous. I'm out of my element here. Any time we've seen each other he's come to me, in the city, where I'm comfortable.

Out here...there's nothing but a star filled sky. We definitely don't have this in Dallas since it's obscured by all the bright lights of the buildings. I tilt my head back reveling in the fact that I'm a small part of this great big universe. Wondering if I look like a small shining speck from above just as they appear from below.

My foot hits something while I'm staring at the sky, and I pitch forward almost dragging Jake down with me. But he grabs me before I hit the ground. I peer up into the darkness, trying to see if anyone saw me. The look of shock splayed on everyone's face is a good indicator they did.

Of course, that would be my introduction to his friends. The clutzy girl that trips over something while holding on to her boyfriend. Wait...when did I start refer-ring to Jake as my boyfriend? We've never said anything about being an item, but I've been exclusively seeing him. I can't do the whole date a few people at once to see if you click thing. It's exhausting and I spent so little time with my dates that I couldn't find anything of substance with them.

Then I swore off dating to work on my career...until Jake. The annoying fool worked his way under my skin and into my heart.

"Do you think they saw me?" I whisper. He knows damn well they did.

"Don't worry," he shrugs. "I've had to almost carry most of these guys to their beds at one time. They won't make a big deal about it."

I wish what he had said was true. As soon as we join his friends, one them says, "That was quite some fall, not graceful at all." He puts his fingers to his chin. "I'd give it a five."

"Randall, can you not mess with her before you've been properly introduced," Jake comes to my rescue.

Ah, Randall. The probability of him getting junk punched tonight has just increased, significantly. The rest of the group tries to hide their laughter. Not because what Randall said, but because they can see the daggers I'm shooting at him with my eyes.

Jake pulls me closer to him, arm thrown over my shoulder. "Everyone, this is Charleigh. And, Charleigh, this is everyone."

"That has got to be the worst introduction known to existence," Marshall yells out. He's not wrong.

He starts pointing at each individual person. "You obviously know me," he winks. But he continues, "You've met Randall, that is Dylan, and the lovely lady accompanying him to the bonfire this fine evening is Rachel."

Rachel waves excitedly. "It's so nice to have another girl in this sausage fest. You have no idea how annoying these guys can get when they are together."

I glance toward Randall. "Oh, I think I do."

Rachel opens an ice chest, motioning me to grab whatever I want. I'm not a huge fan of getting shit-face drunk, so I grab a bottle of water that's been shoved to the bottom. The water is frigid compared to the heat of the night, and I quickly pull my hand out, wiping the excess water on my jeans.

I stand next to Jake, joining in the conversations if I

have something to add. Otherwise, I just listen to the stories from their high school days.

I'm not sure why I was so nervous about coming tonight. They brought me in the fold like I had been a part of the group for years, especially Rachel. She treated me like we've always been the best of friends. Even Randall isn't so bad. But if anyone asks, I'll take that little tidbit to the grave.

Everyone else has already gone home, but I wasn't ready to leave yet. There's just something about the peace and quiet in the middle of this empty field. It's relaxing and gives you time to reflect on your life.

We're lying on a blanket he put down in the bed of his truck. We're cuddled together, my head on his chest, his arm wrapped around me, pulling me close. There are things Jake and I need to talk about, but not tonight. Right now, I just want to bask in this moment of content. Slow country music drifts through the speakers from the truck. Between that and the crickets chirping, I fall asleep in the arms of the guy I'm falling for under the twinkling lights of the night sky.

jake

WAKING up next to Charleigh snuggled against my chest is definitely something I could get used to. I should have woken her up to take her home last night, but I didn't. She looked so peaceful in her sleep, and I didn't want to interrupt that. I pulled the blanket over her and fell asleep to her measured breaths under the starlight.

I've never slept so soundly. I look down at her, still sleeping, and run my fingers through her hair. I'm starting to see how quickly you can fall for someone, or at least start to fall for them. I would do anything for her. Hell, she could even be my forever.

And the way she responded to my every touch yesterday was magnificent. I've never felt so connected to someone, not even with Tonya. In such a short amount of time, Charleigh seems to know what I need exactly when I need it.

I *have* to tell her about Layla. Fear of her being done with me is the only thing holding me back, but she deserves to know. Especially since I plan on being a big part of Layla's life. I'll tell her today. Before we get any deeper into this relationship.

We haven't even defined what we are. Maybe she just wants this to be casual. I haven't seen anyone else since I starting pursuing her. And, I definitely feel more than causal about her.

I feel Charleigh begin to stir. Toes pointing and arms reaching overhead to stretch. She slowly opens her eyes, squinting into the now bright sky.

She sits up so quickly she almost hits my head with her own. "Oh, shit." She looks around confused and wild eyed. "We're still in the field."

"No, really?" I tease. "Here I thought we were in the fanciest of hotels."

"Don't be a smart ass," she smacks my chest with an open palm. "Why didn't you wake me up?"

Shrugging I sit up. "You were sleeping, and looked adorable by the way, so I figured why not have an unplanned campout."

"You know, I don't think I've ever slept outside in my life." She leans over me pressing a quick peck on my lips. "Look at you turning me into a country girl."

I laugh, shaking my head. "Sweetheart, a bonfire and one night of sleeping in the bed of the truck doesn't quite make you a country girl. But, it's a start."

"Whatever," she smirks. "I can call myself what I want, and if I say this makes me at least a little bit country, you'll just have to get over it."

I pull her down on top of me, pressing light kisses on

her neck, as she giggles. My hands roam to the bottom of her shirt and slide underneath, caressing the small piece of skin that is now exposed.

"Jake," she whispers. "I'm not having sex with you in the back of a truck in the middle of a field."

"Who said anything about sex?" I ask. "You should really get your mind out of the gutter."

The laugh that erupts from her mouth is loud and causes her entire body to shake. "Yeah, like your head wasn't already there."

I groan. "You're killing me woman."

"Sorry," she says as a smile takes over her face. "Do you think you can take me home? I feel pretty gross in last night's sweaty, smoke smelling clothes."

"I'll take you to my house so we can both clean up, then I'll take you home. Sound good?"

"Sure," she replies. But I can hear the nerves that have crept into her voice, making it shaky.

I'm sure she's wondering what she'll see when we get there after all the things I've said about my parents. But, if I'm lucky they'll be gone to play golf, or do whatever it is they do on Saturday mornings.

* * *

Luck is definitely on my side because when I pull up to my house, the driveway is empty. I breathe a sigh of relief. Not because I'm ashamed of Charleigh, but because my parents can be utter assholes. I don't want to subject her to their ridiculous views because they aren't my own. If I'm being honest, I'm ashamed of them.

The truck gives a slight lurch as I put into park. I look at Charleigh gauging her reaction to where I live. Her eyes are wide, and staring, at the larger than most house I grew up in.

Gently nudging her shoulder, I ask," Are you ready to go inside?"

She at me in total amazement. "Your house is kind of ridiculous, you know?"

I shrug. There's not really anything else I can do. "It's where I grew up."

We exit the truck and Charleigh doesn't even give me a chance to open the door for her. As we make our way to the house, she studies the landscape. Huge bushes line the front of the house, stopping just below the windows. Trees not only line the driveway, but they are strategically placed so that almost the entire yard is shaded.

I unlock the door and push it open only to hear Charleigh gasp. "You actually live here?"

"Live is a relative term," I say. "I'm usually only here to sleep. Otherwise, I stay away as much as possible."

"Why?" she asks, incredulous. "You have so much space you would hardly even see your parents."

"That's where the problem lies," I sigh. "As much as I try to avoid them, they seek me out. They are always trying to make sure I'm not doing anything that breaks their rules." Rules I think are stupid and hypocritical. They are completely fine with me drinking with my teammates, but associate with someone they don't approve of? And, it's like I'm committing some sort of felony. I don't understand their way of thinking.

I don't want to get into the idiocy of my parents with

her. I grab her hand and lead her toward the stairs and my bedroom. As we ascend them, Charleigh takes her time studying everything she can see. From the sterile white walls, to the sleek modern design of the rooms below us, and the row of family portraits that litter the stairway.

We come to my door and I push it open, wondering for a split second if it's clean. But I remember tidying up before I left to get Charleigh yesterday. And, even if I hadn't my mom would have come in here and done it. Because God forbid it look like someone actually lives in this room.

I grab a towel from the linen cabinet situated next to my bathroom door, and hand it to Charleigh. "You go ahead and take a shower, I'll wait."

"Are you sure?" she asks.

"Yeah, go ahead. I need to find some clothes for you to wear."

As soon as the door clicks shut I begin rummaging through my drawers. I pause on an old *Bush* T-shirt Tonya gave me when we were dating, but quickly decide that wouldn't be a good idea. She wouldn't know, but I do, and I'm not giving her a shirt that my ex-girlfriend gave me. Instead, I pull out a football shirt from when I played at Asheville High and dig through the bottom drawer until I find a pair of sweatpants. I doubt either of these will fit her, but it's all I have.

I slip the clothes into the bathroom, setting them on the floor. I'm surprised she didn't lock the door before she got in the shower. For just a split second I consider joining her for a repeat of yesterday afternoon but decide against it.

With the hum of the water running, I walk to my bed and belly flop onto it. Face buried in my pillows trying to decide how I'm going to bring up the topic of Layla. I'm not even sure where to begin. Will she be livid, or will she understand why I haven't told her yet? Will she understand why I've been scared to tell her? Fear that she'll walk right out of my life without a backward glance.

Less than ten minutes have passed when I hear the bathroom door open and small footsteps approach the end of my bed. "That was quick."

"I just wanted to rinse of," she says. "Besides you don't have any of the hair products I use to tame this unruly hair."

She runs her fingertips over my legs, ass, and they slowly drift up my back until she slides her fingers into my hair. Bending down, she gives me a quick peck on the cheek. I notice she has the towel I gave her wrapped around her body instead of the clothes I put in the bathroom for her.

As much as I want to rip that towel off and have my way with her, I restrain myself. I don't know where my parents are, or how long they will be gone. And, that definitely isn't something I want them walking in on. The springs of bed the squeak as I roll off the bed to grab the clothes out of the bathroom. Placing them in her hands, I don't miss the disappointed frown taking over her face and breaking my heart. I just don't want to give my parents any reason to hate her on sight. And they would definitely not approve if they saw us in any sort of horizontal position.

I pull her close to me and lean down until my lips are pressed against hers. I kiss her once, twice, three times before I pull away keeping this from going any further.

"I'm going to hop in the shower," I whisper, voice low, deep and ragged.

Her cheeks are tinged pink, and she simply nods. A small smile takes the place of the frown it held moments before as she drops her towel to the floor, hoping to get the reaction she wants out of me.

Shaking my head, I turn around toward the bathroom door. She's crazy if she thinks that is going to work on me again. But it doesn't stop me from looking over my shoulder to see her standing there, stark naked, smiling wickedly in my direction. The bathroom door slams a little harder than intended and I groan in frustration. This girl is going to be the death of me.

I turn on the shower, adjusting the water until it's just barely lukewarm, needing the cooler water to calm my hormones. Shampoo is in my hair, bubbles slide down my face and into my eyes when they pop open when I hear a shriek from my bedroom. This cannot be good.

Quickly rinsing the soap out of my hair and eyes, I shut off the water, wrap a towel around my waist, and barrel into my room. Water still dripping off my skin onto the plush carpet beneath my feet.

My mother stands in the doorway, hands on her hips, face beet red. "Who the hell are you?" She's yelling at

Charleigh, not giving her the courtesy of an adult conversation.

"I-I'm Jake's girlfriend," Charleigh stutters.

The term girlfriend rolling off her tongue sends a happy jolt throughout my body. In that moment I know she's as serious about me as I am her. Now isn't the time to dwell on that, though.

Mom shoots daggers in my direction. "Jake doesn't have a girlfriend. If he did, I would know."

"Actually," I mumble. "She is my girlfriend."

"Impossible," Mom stammers. "She is not the sort of girl you date."

I don't say anything. I can't. There are literally no words to combat what just came out of her mouth. It's rare that I'm at a loss for something to say, but that moment has come.

"Excuse me," Charleigh scoffs. "What the hell is that supposed to mean?"

"You *will not* take that tone with me young lady."

Charleigh glances at me expectantly, willing me to say something. But I have no idea what to say. Anything that comes out of my mouth will piss one of them off. This is not how I envisioned the rest of the day playing out.

When I continue to remain silent, Charleigh huffs. "I'm going to wait in your truck. I'm ready to go home." She grabs her clothes, shoes and hurries out of the room.

"For Christ's sake, Jake, put some clothes on," my mom scolds. "I refuse for you to see that girl after today."

"Mom, I'm nineteen."

"And, I still pay your bills," she responds. "Now, get dressed, take that girl home, and come right back here."

I don't say anything. I stomp to the bathroom door and slam it closed. She wants to treat me like a fucking child? I'll act one.

* * *

The drive back to Charleigh's apartment is dead silent. No music, no banter, just the deafening sound of disappointment. I place my arm on the center consul, palm up, hoping she will take it. Hoping I haven't completely fucked everything up.

I pull up in front of her building, and she gets out of the truck before I even have a chance to open my door. Stepping out of the truck, I move to follow her, but she whirls around on me.

"Don't, Jake." Rubbing her temples, she looks completely defeated. "I don't want to talk to or see you right now."

I watch her go. Watch her run to her building, shoulders low and shaking. Shit, I've made her cry. All because I couldn't open my damn mouth against my mother. I'm not going home right now, I can't. Instead, I text the last person I ever expected to go to make me feel better.

Jake: Are you home?
  Tonya: Yeah, why?
  Jake: I need to see Layla.
  Tonya: Okay, come on over.

Jake: And I need some advice. I fucked up yet again.
Tonya: I'll help as best I can.

A small part of me is scared of what she has to say about my situation. But if there's anyone that can help me, it's her.

charleigh

THE AUDACITY OF THAT WOMAN. I can't believe she actually treated me like I'm beneath her or something. I know Jake said they were assholes, but I assumed he was over-exaggerating. And Jake...he didn't even say anything. He just quietly stood there, not once opening his mouth to defend me at all.

I'm still fuming. The only thing that has kept me occupied since I got home thirty minutes ago is pacing the floor back and forth. I tried to sit down and draw. It usually helps me deal with my emotions. But not today. Today, my rage wouldn't let me focus on anything.

My phone dings with a message.

Jake: I'm sorry. Please, talk to me Charleigh.

Charleigh: I don't have anything to say to you right now.

Jake: I didn't mean for you to meet her.

Charleigh: Oh, so I'm not good enough to meet your mother.

Jake: Shit, that came out wrong. I meant she isn't good enough to meet you.

Charleigh: I don't know, Jake. Right now, I just need some time.

My phone starts ringing, and I'm about to toss it across the room to the sofa so I that I won't answer it. But Corey's name on the screen catches my attention, and I answer it.

"Hey, Corey. What's up?" I try to inflect some sort of happiness into my voice, but it sounds too bubbly. Too fake.

"Charleigh, sorry to call you on your day off," he pauses. "But is there any chance you can come into the shop?"

I'm in no mood to deal with customers, much less talk to anyone. But, maybe it'll give me something productive to do, time to think. I need to figure out if I'm going to keep this whole thing with Jake going.

"Sure," I reply. "I'll be there in twenty minutes."

Tossing the phone on the counter, I walk to my room, pulling off the clothes Jake let me wear home. I chunk them to the side, landing near the trash can. I'm not actually going to throw them away, but it's where I feel they belong right now.

The screeching sound of the hangers sliding across the rod in my closet is loud amidst the quiet of my apartment. I shove clothes aside trying to find a tank top. Something that makes me feel empowered, and not as small as Jake's mother did today.

Finally, I find my black tank top with "Lady Boss" written in gold glitter. I pair it with a denim mini skirt, throw on my Converse and head out the door. I don't even spend the time to put on my make-up or do anything with my hair. It's a messy bun kind of day.

* * *

As soon as I open the shop door I understand why Corey called me in to work today. There are people occupying all the seats in the lobby. Some are even standing against the wall, patiently waiting their turn.

Sophia is at the front counter, hair thrown up in a ponytail with a pencil sticking through it. She looks completely frazzled. When she sees me, she sighs with relief.

"Thank God you're here, Charleigh," she mutters. "It's been a crazy day. Adrian called in sick, Corey is booked up the rest of the day, and Bianca is being her usual bitchy self and only taking certain clients." She catches her breath. "I have no training, so I'm exactly zero help."

"Take a deep breath, Nat." I tell her, placing my hands on her shoulders to help her calm down. "No worries. We've got this. Send me whoever is up next on the list."

I'm in my work station, getting everything set up, when an older woman comes in and takes a seat in my chair. She's mid-forties, but she looks sad. Like all the life has been drained out of her.

"Hi, Ms.," I glance down at the form containing all

her information. "Hernandez. How can I help you today? Is there anything in particular you have in mind?"

"Hi, I'm not really sure what I want. I need something for my son."

"Okay, we can definitely do that. What are some of his favorite things.

She gives me a list of sports and activities that he liked, as in past tense. And, already my stomach is knots because this isn't someone who just wants to commemorate her relationship with her son. No, this is a mother in mourning, and it breaks my heart.

I know I always said I wanted to make art and do tattoos that mean something to people. But...I don't know if I'm cut out for this. Not after the way Jake's mom made me feel. And definitely not after the way *he* made me feel.

But, I'll do it. Because this...this moment right here is very important to Ms. Hernandez. I start drawing out some of the things she mentioned, basketball, guitars, and a few other small items. Trying to find a way to integrate them into something cohesive.

In the end, she doesn't really like any of the designs. Instead, she wants a heart on her should blade with his name and birthday. Not the day that he died, but the day he was born. The day that gave him life.

When I'm done, I hand her a small mirror, and she turns it and her body toward the mirror so she can catch the reflection. On her shoulder blade is a heart shaded with blues and grays. Blue because it was her son's favorite color. And gray to signify the pain she feels because he's no longer with her. She looks it over in tears as she remembers the life her son had, the joy he brought into her life, and realization that the pain will never truly fade.

She sniffles, trying to find some sort of composure. "How much do I owe you?"

"Nothing," I reply. "Consider it a gift, an act of kindness." I can't charge her. I can't make her pay for a memory of someone she'll never see again.

She tries to argue with me but I stick to my refusal. I was able to give this mother a reminder of her son. A way for her to always carry him with her.

I clean up my station, getting it ready for the next client. My emotions are all out of whack, and I hope I can get myself under control before the next person walks through that door.

Sophia is at the front counter, giving estimates of how long the wait will be. Some people are happy to wait, while others walk out disgruntled. I pick up the form on top of the pile, but she stops me. Placing a small stack of bills in my hand.

"What is this for?"

"Your last client left it." Sophia sniffles. She either heard the conversation, or Ms. Hernandez told her. "She told me to make sure you took it, and to say thank you for giving her a beautiful tattoo to remember her son."

I nod before walking back into to my room calling for John to follow me. I hope this one isn't as heart shattering as the last.

* * *

It's one in the morning and we're all finally winding down. There are no more customers in the shop. Nobody else wanting a memory forever inked on their skin. I'm tired down to my bones as I help Sophiaclean up the lobby. Help her make sure everything is ready for a new day tomorrow.

Of course, Bianca has to come out of her room and ruin the rest of my night. "Does your uncle know that you did a tattoo for free?" She sneers, putting all of her pettiness on display.

"Last time I checked, that is *my* work station. I can charge what I feel is necessary as long as I pay my booth fee."

"Well," she snorts. "You're never going to make any money if you keep doing shit like that."

Today is not the day for her to give me crap. It's been a long, rough, heartbreaking day.

I throw the broom I'm holding down to the floor. "What the fuck is your problem, Bianca? Why do you hate me so much?"

She stands still, mouth gaping open, in shock. I've never stood up to her, and I don't think she expected it. But, I'm done. I can't take it anymore. If this is what working with her is going to be like all the time, one of us is going to have to go. And it sure as hell isn't going to be me.

Finally, she finds her voice. "N-nothing," she stutters.

"Then why Bianca? Why do you constantly bitch me out for no reason? Why do you have to put me down? Try to make me feel like I'm two inches tall?"

"Because you're better than me, Charleigh."

Sophia is by the front door, wringing her hands together, unsure what to do. Corey comes out of his office, leaning against the wall. I'm going to safely assume that he's not going to do anything to stop this. It's been brewing for far too long.

"How in the hell do you figure that?"

She walks up to one of my drawings hanging on the wall. "Do you not see this? Do you not see how fucking talented you are? It's intimidating. I've been working in this shop for a while, and I knew there would be a day when people would want you to design their tattoos over me."

"That doesn't even make sense. I've admired you since the moment you started tattooing here," I yell. "You are the only one besides Corey that inspired me to continue my apprenticeship. That made me want to do better."

Bianca is quiet for a moment, dumbstruck. "You look up to me?" She asks like it's hard to believe. She is ridiculously talented, but her bad attitude isn't winning her any favors.

"Why do you think I followed you around at the beginning? It's because I wanted to learn from one of the best female tattoo artists in our area." I walk up to her, slowly. Worried she's going to react like a caged animal and attack as soon as I'm near enough. "Look, I know how hard it is for women in this industry at times, but it's never going to get better if we constantly tear each other down."

Her body hiccups, tears streaming down her face.

"I'm so sorry. I let my own insecurities get in the way of everything."

I pull her to me, wrapping her in my arms. I don't know why made her feel the way she does, but it had to have been awful. She may have been horrible to me, but I can't do that to her. It's not the way I'm built.

"It's okay," I whisper.

"It's not," she replies. "I just hope you can forgive me."

I already have. Through all the times she was horrible to me, I tried not to let it affect me. I brushed her words off because that's what they are...words. They can only hurt me if I give them that power. Besides, I don't know what demons she's fighting in her own life.

This moment shines a little bit of light on my day. It may have started out like shit, but finally working things out with Bianca makes me feel a little better and lifts a small weight off my shoulder. Now I just need to figure out what I'm going to do about Jake.

jake

IT'S BEEN TWO DAYS. Two freaking days since I've talked to Charleigh. I have no idea what she's thinking or doing. It's definitely not because I haven't tried getting a hold of her either. My phone has never been on the verge of dying as much as it has since she stormed out of my truck.

Texts, calls, voicemails...they all go unanswered. I've done everything short of showing up on her doorstep. The idea crossed my mind. As in, I was looking to see what flower shops were open at nine at night. But, Tonya and Reaf talked me out of it. They said it would backfire.

Honestly, I'm pretty sure Tonya thought it was hilarious how much of an ass I'm willing to make of myself for a girl. But Charleigh isn't just a girl. She's so much more. Funny, smart, talented, and always positive. Even when other people are jerks to her. I just hope she'll give me a chance to apologize.

Tonya suggested I wait a few days before I show up anywhere she may be, which is why I'm slowly driving by Life in Ink. I can't see her through all the people in the chairs.

She wasn't kidding when she said they've been crazy busy. A lot of the success comes from the fact that her uncle promoted her from apprentice to artist. I'm pretty sure she hasn't put two and two together, but she's the reason they run out of appointments. Word of mouth travels fast when the employees are amazing, and that she is.

The next street will lead me to the highway or another street to go around the block again. I pause, debating which way to go. When the light turns green, I take a right, leading me back to Asheville. I don't really want to show up at her work to talk to her. That's her territory, and quite frankly, I'm slightly terrified of her uncle.

"Thank you, Mrs. Foster," I say as she hands me a bottle of water from the fridge. "I hope I'm not intruding by staying here."

"Not at all," she clasps my shoulder. "You and the other boys are practically my other children."

The day my mother humiliated Charleigh, I went home long enough to grab some extra clothes and came straight here. This feels more like home than anywhere else. And...I didn't know where else to go.

"It won't be permanent," I promise. It's not the Fosters' job to help me get on my feet, but I'm beyond grateful that they're helping in any way they can.

"Oh, sweetie. You stay as long as you need to."

Swallowing past the lump in my throat, I nod. What do I say to that?

A few weeks ago, I put in an application for a job in sales. I've never had to work in my life, but it's time. I need a way to provide for my daughter and find a place to live. They haven't called me back yet, and I'm wondering if I should stop hoping on this one job.

I haven't even told Tonya that I plan on transferring to a university closer to home yet. Possibly even the local college. I don't even care if I can play football, as long as I'm here for Layla whenever she may need me. It may be a difficult road to go down, but she is worth it.

And, I'll be close to Charleigh. If she'll ever speak to me again. If she reacted like that toward my mom's comments, how is she going to accept that I have a child? I'm not saying that her reaction to Mom is unjustified because it is, but I can handle not seeing my parents. I can't handle not seeing Layla. Now that I'm starting to build a relationship with her, I can't go back to the way I was before. I won't go back to being that douchebag.

The water bottle is ice cold, sweat already dripping down the sides, as I stand to go to Marshall's room. Before I leave the kitchen, I turn back to Mrs. Foster. "Hey, Mrs. Foster," I ask. "Does Mr. Foster happen to know of anyone that's hiring?"

She places her fingertips on her chin thinking. "You know, he mentioned the other day they were looking to bring on a couple more apprentices. The work is hard, but I think you would do just fine."

Plumbing is definitely not something I want to

make a career out of, but I don't think working with Mr. Foster would be horrible. It's honest work, and something that may be good for me. My parents never really cared for The Fosters because they see their jobs as something beneath them. From the outside looking in, I can see how horribly flawed and snobby they really are. I'll do everything in my power not to turn out like them

"Thank you," I pause. "I put in a couple of applications around town, and I haven't heard back from anybody. But, I really need a job." My voice is a little shakey, worry creeping in. I really need any sort of job.

"I completely understand, Jake." Her eyes are shimmering, looking at me with a softness that only a mother can. A tinge of sympathy, but also a spark of pride because I'm doing something about my situation. It's the way I wish my mother would look at me sometimes.

Marshall is sitting at his desk, feet propped up next to the computer with a copy of *Beowulf* in his hands. He doesn't even bother looking at me when I come the room and make my way to the little cot they pulled out of the garage so I would have a place to sleep.

The cot is ridiculously uncomfortable. There is no support, just a piece of fabric stretched across the frame to hold my body up. Marshall smirks at me from behind his book.

"What's so funny, jackass?"

"Nothing," he laughs. "You just look funny on that thing. How does your body even fit on there?"

The frame squeaks as I move to find a more comfortable position. "Very, very carefully."

"I don't understand why you don't just sleep on the sofa like a normal person."

"Because," I reply. "I don't want to interfere with your family more than I already have. I feel like a huge inconvenience."

Marshall sets his book down, placing a bookmark between the pages before he lets go of the cover. "How many times have I told you that it's fine you're here? If it were in any way inconvenient, my parents wouldn't have let you stay." He rolls his chair away from the desk. "They look at you as one of their sons. Do you think they would turn me away in a time of need?" He waits for my response and when I only stare at him, he continues. "No, they wouldn't. So, stop moping and welcome to the damn family."

"I get that, but it's still weird." I cover my face with my hands, take a deep breath in, and slowly let it out. "I just feel really shitty, and like I can't do anything right. Charleigh won't talk to me. My parents treat me like an asset instead of a child, and I can't do anything right in their eyes." Placing my hand on my stomach, I take another deep breath, using this moment to cleanse myself of everything that's bothering me. "The only person who is ever happy to see me is Layla, and that's because she's not old enough to know any better. It's only a matter of time until I screw up and let her down."

A cheesy grin takes over his face, and he bats his eyelashes at me. "I'm happy to see you," he says. His voice is high pitched, trying to mimic a girl's, but he's failing miserably.

This is why he's my closest friend. He does whatever

he can to cheer me up, even when I feel like I don't deserve it. We have a friendship as close as the one Tonya and Cami have, and I'm more than grateful for that.

"How about...you don't make eyes at me again," I say, laughing.

"Why?" He bats his lashes again. "Do you not find me attractive?"

"You aren't exactly my type."

"Well, what is your type?" He's digging. He wants me to admit that I have deeper feelings for Charleigh than I've admitted to everyone else but myself.

"Last time I checked, you don't have long blonde hair, or ink on your arms and in other places most people don't get to see."

He lifts the sleeve of his shirt showing off the tattoos Bianca has done for him. "I may not be blonde, but I do have the ink." He winks. The sleeve of his shirt falls, covering his new obsession with tattoos. "You need to call her."

"I've tried. She's not answering." My phone is in my back pocket, digging into my hip. I pull it out, staring at the screen wondering if I should try one more time. Focusing on the take, I do a double take. "Shit," I yell.

Marshall looks over at me, not knowing whether there's bad news on my screen or if I'm continuing my pity party. "What's wrong, man?"

"I'm supposed to meet Tonya and Reaf at a park in Dallas. They want to get a few pictures done for their engagement, and I offered to watch Layla so we can get some one on one time."

"Mind if I tag along, I won't be in the way," he asks. "I

need to get out of this house. That book I'm reading for one of my literature classes next semester is crazy boring. I can barely keep my eyes open while trying to get through the first few chapters."

The legs of the cot slide across the floor as I stand, grabbing my keys off the nightstand between our beds. "Sure, you ready now?"

"Yep. Just need to grab my wallet."

"Let's go then. I don't want to disappoint yet another person in my life." He smacks me in the back of the head while I rub the small of my back. The piece of metal that goes across the cot to support my weight was digging into me. I may rethink sleeping on the couch after all.

* * *

Klyde Warren Park is teeming with families. They dot the expansive lawn playing games, having picnics, and just happy to be in each other's presence. Tonya and Reaf are somewhere having their pictures done. They did the photos of them with Layla before I got here. I'm slowly coming to grips with them being a family unit, but I'm also happy that I didn't have to see the pictures being taken.

Tonya always seems to know how to handle any situation she's put in without pissing anyone off. It's a quality that I admire about her. She's given me more chances to be a better person than I deserve. She's also done really well with mine and Reaf's interactions. Things between us have definitely changed for the better since Christmas.

Layla is pulled tightly against my chest while I go down one of the slides with her. Seeing the toothless smile taking over her face as the wind rushes past us, makes my heart swell. I'm grateful I've been given the opportunity to be in her life when I could have so easy been shut out.

"Are you having fun?" My voice comes out high and shrill. When the hell did I start the whole baby talk thing? Tonya would lose her shit if she heard me talking to her this way. Anytime someone tries to baby talk to Layla, she stops them in their tracks. "Talk to her like you would any other person. She's just like everyone else, just a tinier version." I cannot tell you how many times I've heard her repeat that exact phrase.

Lucky for me...she's not around to scold me. "Do you know how happy you make daddy?" I kiss her chubby little cheeks, bending my head to blow raspberries on her neck. She squirms, making tiny giggle sounds. I assume she's giggling. She makes so many weird little noises that I never know what she's actually doing.

Marshall is sitting on a bench, face glued to his phone. I'm not sure why he wanted to come along. He could have easily texted from the air-conditioned walls of his house. There's no doubt in my mind he's talking to Bianca. I wish he'd tell me what's going on with them, but he's been keeping it quiet.

Tonya and Reaf are walking in our direction, and I stop all the baby talk. I do not want her to unleash on me again about how I'm stunting Layla's speech development. She really needs to put the parenting books down and just let things happen.

Tonya is already talking before she gets to me, while Reaf takes a seat on the bench beside Marshall. "The photographer wants to know if you want some shots of you and Layla."

She's reaching for Layla, and the person I see over her shoulder makes my heart stop. This is not how I wanted her to find out.

Charleigh turns tail, and jogs in the opposite direction. "I'll be back," I say as I place Layla in Tonya's hands.

"Charleigh," I call. "Dammit, Charleigh, let me explain."

But she doesn't stop. She keeps her pace until she's out of sight, and I'm left watching her leave. Wondering if I've lost her for good.

charleigh

I AM SO FUCKING STUPID. I hear Jake's please for me to stop as I run away. Who was that girl standing next to him? Whos baby is that? I'm not even sure how to process what I just saw.

The funny thing is, I was going to the park to get some space from everybody at the shop. And...I was finally going to call Jake back. We needed to have an adult conversation about the situation that happened with his mother, without me stomping off like a two-year old.

I saw him come down the slide with the little girl. I stood there, in awe, and watched them for a few moments, butterflies erupting in my stomach. The scene before me, a small glimpse of what a future would look like with him. It may have been a little early to think that way, but it's no secret that we have one of those rare connections.

I assumed the baby was a cousin or something, but as soon as I saw that girl walk up to him, I knew they were familiar. I could tell the two of them had shared a past.

Hot tears stream down my face, and my nose is runny. I finally slow down three blocks from the park and lean against one of the buildings.

I think back to all the time Jake and I have spent together All the times he texted or came to my place. And I wonder if it was all just an act. Just a way for him to get close to the naïve city girl set on chasing her dreams.

But, he took me to meet his friends, the people spends the most time with. Surely, he wouldn't have done that if he was harboring a secret family, would he? But how can I know? I've never asked him what all he does. As far as I know, he talks to me or hangs out with his friends. Nothing else.

I bury my face in my hands to quiet my sobs as realization hits. Those few times he seemed sad or distant, and unsure. They had to have been because of *her*.

Maybe I'm blowing this whole thing out of proportion. There could be a completely valid reason for him to smile at her like she just made his day. Right now, I can't think of any reason for that to happen. He smiled at her the same way I've seen him smile at me. With that same sort of affection in his eyes like I'm the person he can't live without. That's obviously not true if what I saw today is real.

I'm not sure how I'm supposed to feel about Jake, now. Not sure if anything I felt was real, or if I was caught up in the moment of a possible summer fling with a hope that it could become more.

My phone rings in my purse, vibrating against the

sides, but I make no move to answer it. I'm not ready to talk to him right now. Maybe never again. Instead, I walk the last few blocks back to the shop, trying to rein in my emotions.

I must do a shitty job, though. As soon as I open the door, Corey takes one look at my puffy red eyes and damp cheeks. "What did that little bastard do?"

Shockingly, it's Bianca that rushes to my side before I can answer. She pulls me into her workroom, enveloping me in a hug. I'm not going to lie, this is pretty fucking weird. She is the last person I would expect to come to my defense. Things have been better between us since we had our showdown, but not so great that I would go to her to lean on when I'm upset. It only makes me wonder what all she has dealt with to single me out when I'm hurting and want to help.

"Are you okay?" she asks, gently patting my back.

"I don't know," I say. "Maybe?"

"What happened? I didn't think you would be back already."

"I just," I hiccup. The after effects of the sobs that poured through me on my way back. "I just saw something I wasn't expecting. I don't really want to get into it right now."

Bianca's phone dings from where it sits on the table. Glancing over, I see that it's Marshall. It could be a coincidence, but I have a gut feeling Jake put him up to texting to her to see if I was here. Bianca doesn't grab up her phone the way she usually does to check her message. She chooses to comfort me, and I'm starting to see her in a whole new light.

Slowly extricating myself from her hold, I wipe the tears from my face with the bottom of my shirt. "I can't be here right now." I peer out of her door and see the small group of people waiting in the lobby for their tattoos.

"Can you take on some of my clients today?" I ask. She nods her agreement. "Whoever you can't fit in, see if Sophia can schedule them for tomorrow." I start toward the door adding, "And, let them know I'll give them a discount for the inconvenience.

"I'll ink as many as I can." Bianca grabs my hand and gives it a small squeeze. "Go home and get some rest."

I walk out of her workroom, and right out the front door. Not bothering to give Corey an explanation or tell anybody bye. I get in my beat up Toyota and sit there. A million thoughts running through my head, trying to figure out where I should go.

It's only a matter of time before Jake shows up here at the shop, or at my door. There's only one place he won't know where to find me.

I put my car in drive and turn in the direction of the one person I know will always have my back. The person who will always want what is best for me.

* * *

"I didn't even know you were seeing anyone," my mother exclaims.

That's right. I ran home to mommy. I'm not sorry, or ashamed, about it either. As much as she drives me crazy with the college stuff, she's only looking out for me in the best way she can.

"I know. And, I'm sorry I didn't say anything."

"How long have you been dating?"

"Almost two months?" I'm not even sure. He started invading my thoughts before the first date.

"How in the world did you keep a boyfriend a secret from me for two whole months?" There's hurt in her eyes, and I hate that I put it there. We've always been close. Mom is the first person I would run to when I was having guy problems.

"Well," I start. "You've been on me about the whole college thing, and I didn't have much of a chance to say anything about it. Plus, I'm not sure how things with Jake and I are going to end."

"What do you mean?"

"Summer is almost over, Mom. He'll have to go back to school where he plays football. Where does that leave me?" She begins to speak, but I cut her off. "And the whole reason I'm here right now is because today I saw him at the park with a baby and some other chick. I'm not sure I even *want* to see him again."

The throw pillows lining the sofa fall to the floor as I scoot down to lay my head in Mom's lap. She runs her fingers through my hair, soothing me the way she did when I was a small child. "Did you talk to him about it?"

I don't answer, instead looking at the messages from Jake on my phone.

Jake: Charleigh, where are you?

Jake: Please, just let me explain. It's not what it looked like.

Jake: I've been by the shop and your apartment. I'm starting to worry, and Bianca won't tell Marshall anything.

Jake: Please just reply so I know you're okay.

"Charleigh?" Mom questions.

"No, I didn't talk to him. I ran off and then came here so he couldn't find me."

"Sweetie," her hand stills. "You need to talk to him. I know it's scary, but maybe there's a good reason for what happened today. Besides, if this boy is someone you even think you can have a serious relationship with, which is the case by how upset you are, you need to learn how to talk through your problems."

"I'm terrified, Mom." I sigh. "What if he doesn't feel as strongly about me as I do him? What if I'm not enough for him?"

"Your phone has been making all kinds of noises since you got here. I'm almost certain that you mean a lot to him."

She taps my shoulder, waiting until I'm sitting up before she frames my face with her hands. "Let's get you cleaned up, and then I want you to go home, call him, and talk it out."

I nod. Though her tone is gentle, it's not a suggestion. It's time to put my big girl panties on and deal with what life throws at me.

* * *

The walk up the stairs to my apartment is somber. I'm freaking out on the inside, but mostly I'm just sad. I'm not sure what's going to happen after I call him, but I hope my heart isn't completely shattered in the end.

I stop in my tracks and can't believe what's right in front of me. Jake is slumped against my door, eyes closed as if he's sleeping. He looks like hell. It's only been roughly six hours since I ran from him, but I can tell he's been in turmoil.

One step forward is all it takes for his eyes to open and his head to whip in my direction. "Charleigh." My name is a whispered breath on his lips.

The tears welling up in my eyes can't be helped. I've never had someone sit outside my door waiting for my arrival. "How long have you been here?"

He shrugs. "I don't know. A few hours?"

"Why didn't you go home? I was just about to call you."

He stands up, taking tentative steps toward me. "You weren't answering my texts. I want to explain what happened and didn't know when you would be home. So, I waited." He reaches out a hand to me, hoping I'll take it. When I don't he adds, "Besides, this is a conversation I would rather have in person."

I swallow past the lump in my throat. A part of me wants to turn around, march right down those stairs, get in my car and drive. But the other part, the part that is falling head over heels for him, wants to hear him out.

"Okay," I reach past him, shove my key into the lock, and twist it until I can open the door. "Do you want anything to drink?"

"Please," he says. He doesn't make a move to follow me. Doesn't try to get close to me. He walks to the sofa and takes a seat on the far end. It's weird seeing him in that area. When we came over before, he would sit in the middle until I decided where I wanted to be and adjust accordingly.

I hand the bottle of water to Jake before taking a seat opposite him, not wanting to sit close in case I don't like whatever it is he has to say. "Whos baby were you with?"

"Wow, not even giving me a chance to open my mouth before you hit me with the hard questions." He sets the bottle down without even taking a drink. "That's Layla, my daughter."

My mouth drops open. He has a fucking kid? How did that not come up in any of the conversations we've had? That seems like a pretty big thing to just skip over.

"I know it comes as a surprise to you." His shoulders sag, utterly defeated. "I didn't want to tell you in case we didn't work out. She's a big part of my life, and I was worried you wouldn't be able to accept that."

"I wasn't even given the option to be okay with it." I'm fuming. How dare he assume that I wouldn't be accepting of him having a child. What kind of person does he think I am? "How could you think I wouldn't accept that? She's your child, Jake. I'm not some heartless bitch. I knew you were hiding something, I just didn't know what it was. And while we're on the subject, who was that girl?"

Now is the perfect time to lay it all out there. The second my question registers his back stiffens. My stomach drops, expecting the worst to come out of his mouth.

"She's my ex-girlfriend, and Layla's mother."

"And y'all are just all chummy best buddies?" Jealousy is heard loud and clear in my voice. I can't help it. I might be a tad bit territorial about those I care about. And I care about him deeply.

"Actually, I'm surprised she even lets me have a relationship with Layla. I was pretty shitty to her during the pregnancy." He takes a long drink of water. "Hell, I couldn't even go to the hospital because I was terrified of being a parent. Of turning out like my parents."

"So why was she there while you were having your time with Layla?" I question. I don't mean to sound petty. I really don't, but I've never seen exes with a child get along with some sort of relationship.

"She's always there when I see Layla. I'm not ready to take her on my own yet." I open my mouth to throw in my two cents, but he stops me. "Her fiancé was also there. They were having their engagement photos done, and she came to see if I wanted the photographer to get some of me and Layla."

I'm guessing the pictures with his daughter didn't happen since he spent the rest of the afternoon worrying about and looking for me. Now I feel like an asshole.

"I'm sorry, I shouldn't have jumped to conclusions." I move a bit closer to him. "But, it didn't look good from where I was standing. Also, I'm not happy about the way everything went down with your mother. You could have stood up for me."

"I know, and I'm sorry for that, too. I've never stood up to them in my life. I didn't know how to react."

"That's not exactly an excuse."

"True, but if it makes you feel any better I haven't been home since. I got enough clothes to wear, but that's it."

"Where have you been staying?" Jake moving out of his parents' house on my account is almost enough to make me swoon.

"Marshall's. Where else would I stay? I'm not super close to Dylan, and Randall's home life sucks." Another drink of water. "Marshall is practically my brother. His family took me in, no questions asked."

"That was nice of them."

"I sense a but coming," he says.

"But you still need to say something to them. You're running away from your problems."

"Have I ever introduced you to my kettle?" I shoot him a glare. "I'm just sayin', it seems pretty similar to what you just did."

"We're not talking about me."

"Anyway, I want you to meet Tonya, Reaf and Layla. I think it will ease your mind a bit where they are concerned. Tonya's family is having a cookout and invited me and Marshall. Would you like to come?"

I roll my head back, leaning it on the back of the sofa. "I don't know, Jake. I need to think about everything you've just told me."

He nods, standing up. "I understand." Leaning down he places a soft kiss on my cheek. "I'll text you the address and time. You don't have to let me know if you're coming or not. I'll be more than happy if you show up." His shoulders sag just the tiniest fraction. "But if you don't I'll understand that, too. I want you to know I care about you...a lot. You're my Reaf."

He walks out of my apartment without another word. What the hell did that last statement mean He's so weird sometimes.

The bigger question is do I go, or not?

jake

WAITING the few days between seeing Charleigh and the cookout has been torture. I haven't texted her once, even though I've wanted to so many times. Marshall and Tonya have been the devil and angel on my shoulder. Marshall telling me I should call, and Tonya telling me to let her have some space.

It's weird that Tonya is here for me during my possible breakup with Charleigh. But that's the type of person she is. It used to drive me crazy because I thought people were taking advantage of her, and she was just letting them. But, now I see that she tackles everything with kindness. She gives everyone a chance the same way she gave me one.

My knees are bouncing an unsteady rhythm while we sit around the fire pit. Mr. Burgess is talking about the upcoming college football season. A small part of me weeps about no longer playing football. One look at Layla sitting in her chair away from the fire squashes that feeling. She's the reason I'm doing this. The reason

I'm starting a plumbing apprenticeship and taking online classes in the Fall. Charleigh may be another reason I'm doing it, also. If she'll have me back.

There's a soft tap on my shoulder. Tonya is standing behind me. "There's someone at the door for you." She gives me a small smile before taking a seat next to Reaf.

My feet carry me to the backdoor as fast as possible. So fast that I can't get the damn sliding door open. It keeps getting stuck as I try to push it to the side. Finally, after a few attempts it opens, giving me entrance into the kitchen.

I'm rounding the corner into the living when I hear her voice from behind me. "Looking for someone?"

"How long have you been there?" I ask, mortified.

One hand goes to her hip. "Long enough to see that you don't understand the concept of opening doors."

Groaning, I walk up to her. I reach for her hand, and inwardly do a happy dance when she allows me to hold it. "I was hoping you wouldn't see that."

"Yep, and I'll remember it forever."

"You came." It comes out as a statement and question. I can't believe she's here. I was so sure I would go home tonight with Charleigh no longer in my life.

"I did." She pulls me to her, wrapping her arms around my back. We fit together perfectly, and I bask in this moment. Happy to know that she believes in me. Believes in us.

I lean back just far enough for our eyes to meet. "So, are we okay?"

"I did a lot of thinking these past couple of days. And most of the things are forgivable. So, yeah we're good." I know there's a but coming, and I can't even find it in myself to care. "But, you need to deal with your parents."

"That's on my agenda for tomorrow."

"Agenda? Look at you being all grownup, and adulting."

"I have a kid I have to take care of, I figured it was time."

I pull her back to me, ducking down to capture her lips with my own. I kiss her soft and sweet. Not wanting it to end but pulling away to keep it PG-13 in here. We *are* at my ex-girlfriend's house, and I don't want to make things any weirder than they already are.

"Come on, I want to introduce you to everyone." I pull her to the door leading to the backyard.

"Maybe I should open it since you seem to have problems."

"Smart ass. I'm perfectly capable of opening the damn door." The door glides to the side easily this time. I look over at her and smirk, just in time to see her eyes roll.

Everyone is gathered around the fire trying to look like they aren't busting at the seams to meet my girl. The huge grins on their faces gives away their excitement. Calling her my girl makes me feel proud. Not in any sort of way that means I own, because she owns me completely. Mind, heart, and soul.

"Everyone, this is Charleigh."

Some call out "hi," while others wave enthusiastically. They act like they've never met someone new before. I would call them dorks if it wasn't so funny. Everyone around this fire, they are my family. Even Reaf, as much as it pains me to say it. More so than my parents have ever been.

Tonya is looking at me with bright, shiny eyes, and a smile so wide her face may actually crack. I nod sideways to her, signaling for her and Reaf to join us. Making all the baby noises I want, until Tonya gets over here, I unbuckle Layla from the bouncy seat.

Charleigh hasn't left my side. Her arms are wrapped around her stomach, and I know she's nervous. This is a lot to throw at her at once, but if she's going to be a part of my life, she may as well get used to it. With Layla in one arm, I pull Charleigh closer. "This is Layla, my daughter."

She gasps. "She is precious. Hi, Layla, we are going to have so much fun, and give your daddy a run for his money." Not one ounce of baby talk came out of her mouth. I think her and Tonya will get along just fine.

With Charleigh's hand in mine we walk to meet my baby mama and fiancé. But stop in our tracks when we hear sirens come down the street. That's never a good thing. Even worse when the flashing lights stop in front of Tonya's house.

Mr. Burgess doesn't hesitate to find out what's going on. He bypasses the back door and exits through the gate on the side of the house. I pass Layla over to Charleigh and follow Mr. Burgess to see what's happening.

"What the hell is going on here?" He bellows.

"Sir," an officer replies. "This truck has been reported stolen." He's pointing at my truck. Who in the hell would report it stolen?

Surely, they wouldn't stoop so low as to get the

police involved in our little feud. As soon as the thought crosses my mind their shiny black Mercedes stops in front of Tonya's house. This is beyond ridiculous.

"Officer, this is my truck." His brows furrow. "And those," I point behind him, "are my parents."

"I don't have time for this bullshit," the officer mumbles under his breath.

Me too, I think. I feel Charleigh come to stand beside me, but she's not alone. Marshall stands on the other side of her. Tonya and Reaf are to my right. I look back to the gate and can see Mrs. Burgess's silhouette holding Layla. I'm glad she has my daughter in the back. I don't want my parents to have even a tiny glance of her. They don't deserve it.

"What is wrong with you two?" I march right up to them, no longer worried about disappointing them.

"Do not speak to us that way," my father commands. "You wouldn't come home so we had to take matters into our own hands." He looks around in disgust. "Imagine my surprise to find that you here."

"I thought we told you to handle this whole baby situation." She sneers at Tonya and notices Charleigh. "Oh, that's rich, the girl you impregnated and the girl I caught in your bedroom in the same place. Don't you have any standards, Jake?"

Shocked gasps echo behind me. I'm done with their blatant disregard for anyone's feelings. This ends now. "I am not going to stop seeing my daughter. You are so worried about appearances, but yet you suggested paying Tonya off and me signing over my rights. It will be a cold day in hell when that happens." Mom tries to argue. "No, it's time you listen to me. That little girl over there is one of the best things that has happened to me. Tonya was gracious enough to give me time to get my head out of my ass and be a part of our daughter's life.

"And that girl over there," I point toward Charleigh. "Is my girlfriend. She is also one of the best things in my life. She makes me happy. She makes me want to be a better man."

My chest is heaving, breaths coming out rapidly, but I'm not done. "You will treat them all with respect. And if you can't do that…I will get a restraining order if you come so much as five feet near them. Am I clear?"

My mother has never been speechless in her life, but I've done it. I've given her nothing to argue over. My dad on the other hand is used to getting his way. "Do not expect any help from either one of us. If you stay here, we are taking the truck and not paying your college tuition."

"Take it," I yell. "I don't want the damn thing or your money. I will figure out a way to take care of myself and Layla."

The officers are standing back, heads going left to right as we argue. As if they are watching a ping pong ball being hit back and forth. Sensing we're done, they back away. "We're going to leave, this is a civil dispute." They hightail it to their squad car and pull out of the driveway.

"I'm not playing, Jake." Dad stammers.

"Neither am I." I pull the keys from my pocket and toss them at him. They have controlled my life for far too long. If hurting the people I love is what it takes to earn their affection, I don't want it.

Without a backward glance, I grab Charleigh's hand and lead her once again into the backyard. Tonya, Reaf and Mr. Burgess follow shortly after. The weight of their demands lifts from my shoulders. I feel lighter than I have in years. I wouldn't have been able to put them in their place with Charleigh giving me the courage to do so.

I pull her closer to me, kissing her temple. "I'm sorry you had to see that."

Tonya snorts behind me. "I'm not. That was freaking epic." She looks over at her mom. "Cover Layla's ears." As soon as that is done, she continues. "No offense, Jake. But your parents are complete assholes."

"None taken. It was a long time coming."

We all walk to the hammock set up in the corner. The very one I would spend nights cuddling in with Tonya. It's big enough for all four of us to sit on it. Charleigh and Tonya sit in the middle while Reaf and I sit beside them.

"Layla is getting sleepy," Mrs. Burgess whispers. "I'm going to put her to bed so the four of you can talk."

Leaning forward I place a kiss on her tiny hand. "Goodnight, Baby Girl."

"I'll be in later when she wakes up," Tonya says.

"Soooo," Charleigh drawls. "That was intense."

"That's putting it lightly," Reaf mutters.

"What are you going to do about school?" Tonya asks. "There's no way you can afford tuition when you don't even have a job."

I glance at Marshall who is on the phone speaking in whispers. Going back to college in a couple of weeks is going to destroy him. But thanks to his family, I'm not so worried about my future.

"Actually," I reply. "I do have a job." Both Charleigh and Tonya whip their heads in my direction. "I start working with Mr. Foster on Monday. I've also already started the paperwork to transfer my credits to Asheville Community College."

"That's amazing," Tonya exclaims.

"So, you're staying?" Charleigh whispers. "For good?"

I pull her closer to me, kissing right beneath her ear. "You won't be able to get rid of me now."

She smacks me in the chest but snuggles closer to into my body. "I get what you meant the other night when you said I was your Reaf." She gestures between the two of them. "They are sickeningly sweet together. Almost enough to make me gag."

"I heard that," Tonya laughs.

Who would have thought almost a year after finding out Tonya was pregnant we would be comfortable hanging out with each other? Not to mention having the people we're with beside us. I've come so far from the guy I was last year, but I still have a long ways to go.

Two Months Later

THE STATE FAIR is something I always looked forward to when I was a little girl. The food, sounds, and rides drawing me to them like a June bug to the light. It is definitely one of my favorite places. There are so many different people here. Couples with the beginnings of love surrounding them, families making memories, and those that are just here for the food.

We are here to make memories. Tonya and I thought it would be fun to do a big outing and bring Layla to the fair. We know she's not going to remember any of it, but I want fair food.

It's a rare Saturday off work for me. It's one of the busiest days at the shop, but I pleaded with Corey to let me have the day. If we get done in time, I'll go in when we're done. Bianca is slowly working her way to becoming one of my closest friends. She's been down lately because Marshall isn't here. He wanted to try the long-distance thing, but she said it'd be too hard with their conflicting schedules. I feel awful for her, but I know she did what she thought was best.

We haven't heard a peep from Jake's parents since that night at Tonya's house. Good riddance. It's a wonder he's turned out decent being raised by them. I've never felt so cherished as the moment he stood up for both me and his daughter. We went back to my apartment that night and he didn't leave until late Sunday night.

I take a moment to watch Layla, seeing how she reacts to energetic buzz of her surroundings. This child is going to be a trouble maker when she gets older. The noise and lights don't seem to phase her. If anything, she's completely enamored by it all.

Turkey leg in hand, we come across my favorite ride. "Want to ride?" I ask Jake.

The size of this Ferris wheel is exponential compared to the one at the carnival we went to, and he stares the ride down as if it's offended him. "I'm not going to pretend that I want any part in that." He pulls Layla from Tonya's arms. "Y'all go ahead. Baby Girl and I will stay down here. Safely on the ground."

I'm not sure where we're heading in our relationship, but I know I love him with every inch of my soul. "That's fine with me." I glance toward Tonya, "Do you want to ride?"

"Sure," she shrugs.

Jake's shoulders steady me as I lean into him on my tiptoes. "Love you, scaredy cat," I whisper. Giving him a quick peck on the cheek, and Layla's hand a tiny squeeze, I turn toward the entrance.

"I'll see you at the end," I call back.

Jake comes into view just before we hand our coupons over to the ticket taker. What in the world is he doing over here?

Tonya's eyes go wide when she doesn't see Layla. "Is everything okay? Where's Layla?" Worry about her daughter has panic creeping in. Her voice high and shrill.

Jake laughs, "She's fine. Reaf has her."

"So, why are you here?" I ask.

He eyes the ride once again, doubt in his eyes, before shaking it off. "I want to ride with you."

"I'm sorry, did I hear you correctly? You want to get on the 'death trap' as you called it?" I'm being a smart ass about it, but I know how he feels about heights. There's no way he's going to get on this much bigger ferris wheel.

"Yep." He gets behind Tonya and playfully pushes her out of the line. "Sorry, Tonya, but I need some time with Charleigh."

"Whatever," Tonya rolls her eyes. "I'll just go sit over there, in the nice cool shade while y'all are sweating your as-, I mean butts off."

Jake shakes his head, and mumbles, "She's taking this no swearing thing way too far."

"I heard you. And, when your daughter calls someone a jackass, you'll understand," she calls back as she walks to the bench Reaf and Layla are occupying.

Passing the coupons to the ride operator, we get into our seat, waiting for him to latch the bar. "She really needs to lighten up."

"Well," I say. "She has a point. You don't want to be the parents of the foul-mouthed kid in school."

"I guess," he mutters.

The ferris wheel begins turning and we glide backward. Jake is doing his best to not look down, keeping his eyes closed, but I can see the beads of sweat begin to form on his forehead. Every time the ride stops to let someone off he grips the bar tighter.

We are slowly making our way to the top of the ride, and I'm worried he's going to freak out like he did last time. The time on this ferris wheel is so much longer than the carnival due to the massive size.

Finally, we are at my favorite part. I can see the Dallas skyline perfectly, and even through the smog it is breathtaking. The warm afternoon air is gently lifting the ends of my hair and position myself to help Jake calm down. Ready to distract him at a moment's notice.

His hand is shaking in my own. But when I glance up, his focus is on my face, waiting for me to meet his eyes. He pulls something out of his pocket with his free hand, almost dropping the tiny velvet bag.

"What is that?" I nod toward the hand trembling in his lap. I hope that's not what I think it is. I'm not sure I'm quite ready for that step yet.

"It's not what you think, not entirely," he says. "So, you can get that terrified look off your face."

A shaky laugh escapes my lips. "Um, okay."

"Charleigh, you are the absolute best thing that has happened to me. I would still be under my parents' thumbs if it weren't for you," he pauses. "You've taken all the craziness in my life and accepted it. Accepted Layla, and the friendship I need to have with her mom in order to co-parent effectively."

I swallow hard, tears forming in my eyes. If this isn't a proposal, what the hell is it?

He pulls a thin gold band out of the bag, holding it between his forefinger and thumb. It has two hands meeting in the middle around a small diamond. My eyebrows scrunch together.

He pulls our entwined hands to his lips, and gently kisses the back of mine. "This is a promise ring. We aren't ready for marriage. I know that, and so do you. This ring is a promise. A promise to continue bettering myself, and always work my ass off to be the man you deserve. A promise that somewhere down the line, when we're ready, I'll ask you to be my wife. A promise that my heart will always be yours."

I don't say anything. I can't. I don't have any words to express the happiness swirling through my veins. This boy, no *man*, who I had no intention of falling for is by far the sweetest person I've ever known. My heart warms at the promises he's making to me, and I want nothing more than to get off this ride and show him how much he means to me.

"Charleigh?" He asks when I still haven't uttered a word. "You don't have to accept it. It's not going to change anything I've said."

I grab the ring from his hand to put it on my finger, jostling our chair. Jake grips the bars, eyes wide until it stops swaying. "A simple okay would have been fine."

Scooting closer, I throw my arms around him,

burying my face in his neck. "I'd be crazy not to wear it after that kind of declaration. I love you, Jake."

"I love you, too," he mutters into my hair. He pulls back searching my eyes. Looking for any doubt hidden within them. He won't see them. I have zero doubts when it comes to him.

He leans in, bringing his lips to mine. The moment so similar to our first kiss. Only this time, he initiated it. He pushed his fear of heights aside to make this special for me. A moment I'll remember forever.

I break the kiss as the we start to descend. "Thank you. This," I gesture around us, "means so much to me."

He squeezes my hand and we're enveloped in a comfortable silence. Happiness and love filling the air around us. I can't wait to get off this ride and show Tonya, as weird as that may sound. But, I know she'll be happy knowing Jake has someone to lean on.

We may be the most unconventional family unit known to man, but I wouldn't trade them for the world. I wouldn't have formed a friendship with Tonya or realized that I could have a career and love, if I hadn't given Jake a chance. I look forward to everything our future may bring.

* * *

Prologue

The mirror in the bathroom is foggy from the shower. The towel leaves streaks across the glass as I wipe it to see my reflection. Blonde hair in stringy wet tendrils, eyes wide with nerves and excitement.

The Fall semester starts in a week, and this is the last time I will be able to see *him*. I wasn't looking for a relationship over the summer. But he charmed me and made me laugh. I thought it was going to be just a fling. One last hoorah before I started over in a new town. Not that I had any sort of relationship prior to him. Nobody goes for the geeky, quiet girl.

I blow dry my hair, trying to decide what I'm going to wear tonight. A pink sundress hangs over my door, but I don't think I want to wear it anymore. I want tonight to be special...for both of us.

As soon as I shut the blow dryer off, I walk into my room and head straight for the walk-in closet. It's not huge, but it's a decent size. I don't have enough clothes to fill it. On the right side, my fandom t-shirts hang in all their glory. Everything from Harry Potter to the Walking Dead. Jeans line the shelves below them. On the left, and the emptiest area of my closet, hang the very few dresses I own. Aside from the dress hanging on my bathroom door.

I slide the hangers to the side, searching for the perfect dress. Too plain. Too blah. Pushing over three more dresses, I find the perfect one. It's the one thing all girls have in their closets. The little black dress. The last time I wore mine was during my induction into the honor society.

The floor is littered with sneakers, Vans, and Converse. I know there are a few pairs of heels in here somewhere. I shuffle through the shoes, throwing them aside. It looks like a mine field in here. Finally, I find the black heels I'm looking for. Inspecting them, I'm not that crazy about wearing them. But, they are the only pair I have so they will have to work.

Shoes in one hand, I use the other to pull the dress off the hanger and place them on my bed. My curling iron is plugged in and heating up. I open my makeup case and study the few contents in there. Mascara, lip gloss, and eyeshadows in neutral colors.

I don't bother with the eyeshadow or lip gloss. Instead I sweep the mascara onto my lashes, then go to Mom's bathroom. She has so much makeup. I don't even know what half of it is, but I spot a tube of lipstick and grab it before heading back to my room.

The curling iron slides to the bottom of my hair easily. Forming small waves at the ends, just enough to give my hair a little bit of bounce. I open the tube of lipstick. It's bright red. I've never worn this color before, and I'm not sure I can pull it off, but I put it on anyway.

The girl looking back at me in the mirror is not the one I was before getting ready. The bright lipstick makes me feel more mature and confident. Like I can conquer the world.

Rushing down the hall, I call out, "Mom, Dad. I'm going out, I'll be back later."

"Okay, honey," Mom says from the kitchen. "Be careful."

"I will." That's the thing about being the good, nerdy girl. Your parents don't even bother asking where you're going. They just assume it's to meet up with friends from various school clubs. I've never even had a curfew.

Grabbing my keys, I walk out the door, and practically sprint to my car. Ready to see the guy that's stolen my heart.

* * *

It's ten 'til seven when I pull up to the restaurant. This place is packed. How are we even going to get a seat?

After parking the car, I take one last look in the visor mirror, making sure my lipstick hasn't smudged. There's a bench right outside the restaurant and I take a seat to wait.

Twenty minutes later I still haven't gotten a response. Maybe he's stuck in traffic or can't find his keys. I text him, hoping he'll answer.

Darcy: Are you almost here?

Another ten minutes go by, then thirty, and still no response. Tears are welling up in my eyes, but I refuse to let them fall. I can't believe he stood me up. He's always been early. I don't understand. Was he just playing me?

Barely containing my sadness, I march to my car, unlock the door, and slide into my seat. The second the door is closed, I let my sobs free. Let all the emotion welling up inside me find their way out through the hot, salty tears streaming down my face.

Another half hour has passed before the tears begin to slow, and anger takes control. I was so stupid to think someone like him would ever want someone like me. He's attractive, athletic, and the complete opposite of who I am. The shy, meek girl. The one nobody truly sees.

With a new resolve, I put the key in the ignition and

start my car. I leave for Hilltown University next weekend. It's time for a change. I will not be the girl everyone sees through. Don't get me wrong, I'm not going to be a party animal either. But, it's time for my nerdy ways to hit the road.

Never again will I let someone make me feel the way I feel tonight. He may have broken my naïve heart by not showing up, but he is also the catalyst to a new and improved version of me.

Pick up your copy of *Remember That Night*

acknowledgments

You know that old saying, "It takes a village?" That's not only true in raising children. I couldn't have finished this book without my amazing village. I want to say thank you to my Alpha readers: Jennifer, Mistee, Carine, Cynthia, Cass, and Kristin. Your excitement and demands to write faster helped me finish this book. My fellow sweet writers: Tasha, Heather and Sadie; our conversations help me get through the day. I'm so happy I've connected with y'all. I hope we have many years of cheering each other on and building each other up. Jessi, I wouldn't have finished this book on time if it weren't for your daily encouragements. Victoria, I literally do not know what I would do without you. You, my friend, are amazing and I bow down to your awesomeness. KP Designs, thank you so much for bringing my characters to life on the cover. It's absolutely stunning. Shelly, thank you for whipping my books into shape. Even when they are much later than I said they would be.

My sisterhood gals. You make every day better. Y'all are some of the most supportive ladies I know. Keep being awesome. And Casey...I worked that damn pretzel thing into my book. Pretzels are delicious, but I still love you.

Mom and Dad. Thank you for raising me to be a

dreamer. And, not rolling your eyes every time I complained about how much trouble this book was giving me. Your support means the world to me.

Nessa, you're my girl. My sister from another mister. Life would be dull without you in it. Thank you for being supportive and my personal cheerleader. Besties for life, yo.

Hubs, Boy Child and Wee One. You give me inspiration every single day. Thank you for not complaining about fend for yourself nights so I could write. And Wee One, thank you for telling me to get my butt in the chair and write. I wish for nothing but amazing things for y'all. May all your dreams come true.

Readers and bloggers. Because of you I continue to pour my heart into these stories. Thank you for taking a chance (see what I did there) on a newbie author. You're excitement means everything to me.

And last, but not least, my reader group the Dreamers. I love talking to y'all on a daily basis. You've given me books to add to my TBR and helped me with names whenever I'm stuck. Thank you for being so awesome!

www.ingramcontent.com/pod-product-compliance
Lightning Source LLC
Chambersburg PA
CBHW030633190726
48286CB00008B/2507